PETALS OF DECEPTION

Glenda Yarbrough

Other books by Glenda Yarbrough
Under The Fish Pond
What Happened Last Night
Little Things
The Shooting
Thomas Matthew

Petals of Deception
Published by GG Publisher
Copywrite 2012 glenda yarbrough

Acknowledgement:
It is with deep appreciation that I write the words thank you to Ruth Wilhite, Andrea Brown and Sandra Roden in helping me with Petals Of Deception, not only for their encouragement, but also for telling me the difference between then and than and a few other things.

Book Cover's Rose: Courtesy of Barbara Frances Kelsoe Wynn's rose bush.

Dedication

This book is for my granddaughter, Rachel Wilhite. Not only did God give you beautiful red hair and sparkling blue eyes, but He gave you a loving spirit and a zealous independence.

Chapter One

The golden velvet rose petals were soft and delicate to the touch as she inhaled its subtle fragrance. Mary Ellen Forsman cradled the long stemmed rose in her hand before laying it on the round antique table. The table sat in front of the living room window with long white lace curtains. This was a perfect setting for the rose.

It was so romantic that Harvey would do this, but she never imagined he would leave a beautiful rose lying on the front porch. Coming by so early this morning while she slept, just to leave her a rose. Wonder what time he was here? It would've been nice to see him. Last night he had been here, but she cherished each moment with her future husband.

In two weeks they would be married, but two weeks seemed so far away. She wished it were now. Oh, the joy of true love.

A smile touched her lips. "You're worse than some sixteen-year old on her first date," her mother said last night when she stood on the front porch watching Harvey walk down the sidewalk to his car. She would have walked with him, but her mother had hissed her remark at her through the screen door.

Ok, so she acted like some sixteen-year old. Who

cared if she was thirty-four? When Harvey looked into her eyes, the depth of her soul rose to her heart in such a flutter that her spirit felt as if it would fly from her chest. Her heart beat fast, her knees went weak. She actually got weak just because he looked at her. Wasn't that what she had always read that love was supposed to be like? In the romance novels she read, the man was always manly and the woman weak kneed as she was swept away in a passion of burning love.

She didn't care if he was forty-eight, had a receding hairline. He was hers. And that made her heart beat faster. Never before had she been able to say some man was hers. She had never been married, nor had there ever been anyone in her life. But what no one knew, not her mother, not even Harvey—she had never been kissed until Harvey kissed her one night right on the front porch. In all her years, there were no moonlight walks, or kisses under the stars, no snuggling on a rainy day. Nothing.

His kiss was the sweetest kiss—there could have never been a sweeter kiss—just couldn't be. Electrifying. It was so soft, sweet, tender, yet full of fire. It was as if these passionate emotions that had been lying dormant all her life were now awakened. Never did she want to be alone again.

Lust had never been in her life before, but this feeling was so wild, for a moment afterward she felt guilty. Perhaps she had sinned, she thought. This was nothing like what she thought love was like. The married couples she saw, went to church with, or even saw at the mall—never gave any indication they were having these kinds of feelings. Oh, sure, in the movies, yeah, but right there on her front porch! She never dreamed she would feel such.

But she always did when she thought that in two weeks

she would be Mrs. Harvey Broyhill. She would be in bed with her husband. The idea caused her to blush. She blushed even now just thinking about it.

She was a virgin, but she knew what would happen on their wedding night. She may never have been exposed, but she knew—she read books—she watched TV. It gave her goose bumps when she thought about it.

She picked the rose up and held it to her nose. She wondered if Harvey ever got goose bumps when he thought of her—of their first time.

It wouldn't be his of course; he had been married before. His wife, Mildred, died last year. They were married almost thirty years, but even if he hadn't been married before, most men didn't wait. But she didn't want to think about that.

Would she have waited if she had had someone? She thought so, but still she questioned it. Would she have enjoyed the pleasure of love on some wild summer night under the stars if she were madly in love in her teens? Or even her twenties? But there had not been anyone who ever even asked her out. Why, she did not know. She wasn't dog ugly. But she was quiet—to the point of shyness that left her speechless in a crowd. There were no close boys as friends in high school, and her girls friends never offered to fix her up with some friend of their boyfriends. All she did was go to church with her parents, school, and take piano lessons.

She laid the rose down and turned for the kitchen. There should be a vase in there; under the sink would be the most likely place. The door creaked as she opened it. Her mother sat at the kitchen table with a bowl of cereal in front of her.

"If you would let me, I would fix you something to eat."

"No. This is fine. I don't want to be a bother," Gladys Forsman replied.

Gladys always said this when she wanted to be humble. It was a game she played. Mary Ellen hated this game! Why didn't she just say no or yes and leave out the 'I don't want to be a bother' business?

She removed the vase from under the sink. "It's no bother if you want something."

"I'm fine. What are you doing?"

"Oh, Harvey left the most beautiful yellow rose on the porch. I'm going to put it in a vase." She ran cold water into the white bud vase, as she did, she touched the pink roses on the vase. Her daddy had given her a rose in this vase when she'd turned seventeen. He said in one more year she would be a young woman, and he wanted to give her flowers before all those boys beat him to it. Then he had smiled at her. A warm loving smile. He was a private man, saying little.

But no boys brought her roses, and very few came calling. Perhaps she should not have been so shy, but she really couldn't help it. She was just being herself.

"How come he left it out on the porch?"

"I don't really know, other than perhaps we weren't up when he came by."

"Looks to me like he should have waited until tonight so he could have given it to you in person. A dog could have carried it off."

"I don't think so. We don't have a dog."

"Well, he doesn't know anything about the neighbors' dogs. Especially that new little pup next door. Have you seen him? He's nothing but a pest. I had my house shoes sitting on the back porch to dry from the morning dew, and that little devil was carrying them off. I just happened to see him! No telling where he would have carried them or how bad he would have chewed them up. A pest, that's all he is. If I catch him back over here again..."

"What do you think we should have for dinner? I thought I'd call Harvey and tell him to come in time to eat. I only have four students this afternoon, and I thought perhaps we could have an early dinner."

"Makes no difference to me. He's your guest."

Mary Ellen turned, staring at her fifty-nine year old mother. Daddy has been dead now for ten years, and she never hinted at another marriage. Satisfied to just sit in this house day in and day out, watching her soaps. Oh, how I hate those soaps! silently Mary Ellen screamed as she gave a small shake of her head.

"What are you shaking your head about?"

"Nothing."

"I saw you! Don't stand there telling me 'nothing'."

"It just seems like nothing matters to you. You get up, eat your breakfast, watch your soaps. All day. Don't you ever want to just get out there and live?"

"Ha. This coming from the big getter outer."

"You don't have to be sarcastic."

"I'm not. I just don't see you setting the world on fire. Oh, I forget...you're the one getting married in two weeks."

"Mother?" Puzzlement filled Mary Ellen's voice. Gladys had never said anything like that before.

"What?" Gladys ate another spoonful of cereal.

"What's wrong with you this morning? If I didn't

know better, I would think you didn't like Harvey."

"What's not to like. He's got a good job, kids grown, and got most of his hair."

Oh, she didn't have to make that hair remark!

Mary Ellen knew what she was really saying. That he was dull! As if the only good thing about him was his job and no kids to raise. Gladys couldn't see the gentle loving man that she saw. Nor the fire he set ablaze within her.

She turned away. She didn't want to blush in front of her mother.

Mary Ellen retrieved the rose from the table in the front hall. Walking back into the kitchen, she asked, "Have you thought about how it's going to be once I move out?"

"No. You ain't gone yet. There's many a slip between the cup and the lip."

"What! What's that supposed to mean?"

"Just an old saying." She ate the last bite of her cereal. "I'll worry about that when I have to—when the time comes."

"Well, it's almost here...and I don't need any old saying."

"But not yet, you got two weeks." She rose from the table, pulled her housecoat closer to herself. "I'm going upstairs and take me a nice warm bath. Maybe I just might go for a walk."

"You're going to miss your Soaps?" Mary Ellen gasped.

Gladys shrugged, turned and went up the back stairs.

Now what was that all about?

Mary Ellen sat the rose in the middle of the dining room table, then picked up the morning paper, flipped to the TV section. Hum! Just as she thought. The morning soaps weren't coming on—there was a special. A space flight was being shown.

She lifted her eyes up toward the ceiling, and again gave a small shake of her head, then went into the hallway to call Harvey.

"Tonight at six? That would be nice. Yeah, I'd like that. Is there anything you want me to bring?" Harvey asked.

"No. I'll take care of it. How about baked chicken, smothered in mushroom sauce?"

"Good."

She smiled. "All right. I'll see what else I can come up with." Nice salad, greens peas, corn rolls. The menu was forming in her mind. "Then I'll see you tonight."

"Yes, at six."

"Alright." She didn't really want to hang up the phone, but she knew he had work to do and she had lessons to prepare for her piano students, who would be coming at three. She had a full day before their arrival, and everything had to be perfect for dinner. Then she remembered. "Oh, yes…thank you for the rose."

"What?"

"The rose…the yellow rose."

There was silence. Then he asked, "What yellow rose?"

"The one I found on the porch."

He gave a low chuckle, slightly embarrassed as if he had done something wrong. "I didn't leave you a rose. I kinda wish I had now…" But it would never be yellow roses, Harvey thought to himself. Never.

"If you didn't…"

Who could have left such a lovely yellow rose?

Chapter Two

Mary Ellen heard the front door shut and looked up from the books lying in her lap. Her mother removed her sweater and hung it on the coat tree in the front hallway. Mary Ellen looked at her watch. Thirty minutes. Nice walk. At least that was a good start.

"How was your walk?" she asked as her mother walked into the living room.

"Fine. I saw Alice Petrie near the park. She was sitting on a bench feeding those silly birds. I don't see any pleasure in feeding a bunch of freeloaders."

"What?"

"Those birds. They're too lazy to get out and look for food. Course they don't have to when you've got fools like Alice Petrie sitting there pitching food at them. Just a bunch of freeloaders—begging for food. Stupid birds."

"Mother! They're birds. I thought that's what you believed birds did—letting the hand of God feed them."

"Alice Petrie ain't God," she rebuked.

"You have been in such a nasty mood all morning. Are you sure you're alright?"

"What? I'm in a nasty mood just because I don't like freeloading birds! What's that got to do with my mood."

"That's not what I mean. This morning at the breakfast table, you seemed as if something was on your mind—that you were upset—just not yourself."

"What's there to be in a good mood about? What's there to be in a bad mood about? I'm not in any mood. I just don't see things like everyone else. Birds ought to have to look for their food. Make their own way. Who's supposed to take care of them? They—ah—never mind. If that old fool wants to spend her day feeding birds, let her."

She moved toward the kitchen. "Any tea in the refrigerator?"

"I think there was a little left from last night. Harvey drank a glass, but there was plenty left in the pitcher when I put it back in the refrigerator."

She heard the cabinet doors open, glasses rattling, then the cabinet door slammed, and the refrigerator door opened. In her mind's eye, she could see her mother bent over the open door, head inside the frig as she moved items around, searching for the tea. The tea pitcher was sitting on the second shelf—the same place it always sat.

Sometimes she worried about her mother. She wasn't an old woman—what had happened to make her old before her time? She had always had a fairly comfortable life, never worked outside her home. Her husband brought home his paycheck, turned it over to her to manage, and she had led a quiet, comfortable life. But in the last few years she seemed to age beyond her years.

She didn't want that for herself. To be old before she had a chance to first be a young bride. But who was she kidding? She wasn't a young bride. A first time bride, but not her husband's first bride.

No, she scolded herself, those thoughts weren't

allowed. She loved Harvey and it would not have made any difference if he had been married twelve times—he was her husband this time and that was all that mattered.

"I don't see any tea."

"It's on the second shelf." Same place as always.

"Well, I still don't see it. Are you sure there is any tea?"

"Yes, mother. If you didn't drink any after Harvey left, there is tea. I didn't drink it."

"Well, I sure as heck didn't. And it ain't here. Maybe Harvey drank more than you thought. Maybe he finished it off when he brought that rose."

She got up from her seat, laid the books in the chair and walked into the kitchen, coming up behind her mother, whose head was still in the frig. "Let me see." Mary Ellen touched her mother's shoulder, and she stepped aside.

"Well, see…" Gladys swept her hands in grand gesture to the opened refrigerator door.

"Here." Mary Ellen handed Gladys the tea pitcher.

"Where was it?"

"Right where I told you."

"Now don't take that tone with me! Just because you're getting married in a couple of weeks and having roses left on the door step don't mean you can take that tone with me."

"I don't have a tone. I just have lessons to prepare."

"What did Harvey say about the supper?"

"He's coming."

"And the rose? How come he sneaked it on the porch before daylight?"

"He didn't sneak it on the porch before daylight."

"Well, whatever time he sneaked it there."

"He didn't sneak it at all."

Her mother looked at her over the tea glass. "What do you mean? He didn't sneak—or he didn't put it there."

"He didn't put it there."

Her mother coughed, strangled on the tea. She coughed—again—again, and she tried to breathe, but she couldn't for coughing. Her shoulders heaved, gasping for air! Mary Ellen patted her back.

"Who—in heaven's name—left it than?" she finally managed to say.

"I have no idea."

"None?"

"None."

Her mother sat down at the table. She sat there for a moment, deep in thought. She said her words slowly, selecting them carefully. "You know...this sounds silly, but what if—and mind you I am saying what if. But what if it's from your father?"

Mary Ellen turned and stared. Her mouth fell open—a hard stare upon her face, her hands resting on her hips. Her mother has finally gone over the edge! Gone mad at fifty-nine. Oh, God in Heaven, don't let me go mad at fifty-nine—or any age. Don't let this happen to me!

"Don't look at me like that!"

"Have you gone stark crazy mad! How can you say such?"

"We don't really know what happens at death," Gladys replied matter of fact. "How do you know your daddy didn't ask God to let him come back to earth to give you a flower to celebrate your wedding?"

Mary Ellen glared at her mother. She couldn't believe this. "Listen to what you are saying. You're talking like a crazy woman." She quickly added, "And no, I didn't say you were crazy, just talking like one."

"Stop saying that. Just get out of my way, Miss Know It All. You tell me where it came from. You got more than one beau—someone you failed to tell your old mamma about? I didn't think so." She took her glass, waving Mary Ellen aside. "Just let me drink my tea in peace." She moved to the sink, leaning against it as she drank the tea.

Gladys then looked at her daughter through the top of the glass as she titled it upward. Just before she took a drink, she said, "I hope you didn't mention that rose to Harvey."

Of course she mentioned it to Harvey. How else would she have known he didn't sent it? "What are you getting at?"

Gladys lowered the glass. "Well, he might wonder just where that rose came from. Especially since you don't think it came from your daddy. Maybe there is some young whipper-snapper out there that is making his move before you get married."

"Oh please, mother. Just like there has been all these men knocking on my door."

How could her mother say such? She whirled around and went back into the living room and picked up the music books. The open book lay in her lap, but she couldn't focus on the words.

"Now, Mary Ellen, you know I didn't mean that." Gladys walked into the room. "I was just mouthing off. I'm sorry, Buttons." She offered a slight smile, her head tilted toward Mary Ellen.

Buttons? That was the pet name father always used for her. She was only calling her Buttons trying to make amends for those horrible words. She was just using it to patronize her.

"You know I want you to be happy. I know you didn't just move in on Harvey. I know if he had not made the first move—you would still be an old maid sitting here."

"If that was to make me feel better..."

The front doorbell buzzed. Her mother sat the tea glass down on the piano and moved toward the front door.

Why did she sit that tea glass on the piano? She knew how much I detested any type of wet glasses sitting on my piano!

Gladys opened the front door. From where she was sitting, Mary Ellen could see a deliveryman standing on the front porch, a package in his hand.

"Yes?" Gladys questioned.

"I have a package for Miss Mary Ellen Forsman."

"Mary Ellen," Gladys called over her shoulder.

"Just sign for it, mother."

Gladys signed the man's clipboard, took the package, and closed the door. She picked her tea glass up from the piano and handed the package to Mary Ellen.

"Who's it from?"

Gladys shrugged her shoulders. "There's no name. Open it."

Mary Ellen shook the square package. It was about twenty inches by twenty inches, wrapped in brown paper.

"Don't shake it. There might by something in there that might break."

"No, I didn't hear anything move. What do you think it is? Or from who? I just don't like this. First the rose, now this. What does it mean?"

"You won't listen to me. I gave you my thoughts."

Mary Ellen shook her head. The one person, who should be of help, was talking foolishness.

Slowly she ran her hand over the package, searching for some mark that would identify who sent it. There was nothing on it but the her name and the name of the delivery company. This company shipped anything from anyone. That told her nothing. Maybe if she called the company...

"Open it."

Her hands shook as she tugged at the taped ends. The brown wrapper fell away and a large box of fine chocolates was exposed.

"Oh, my!"

"Is there a card?"

Mary Ellen looked inside the brown wrapper. "No. Nothing. Just the candy. But who is doing this?"

"Let me see." Her mother took the box and inspected it closely. "Godiva Candies. Fine chocolates. Oooh—and they are! They make wonderful chocolates." She gave the box back to her daughter. "You going to open it now?"

"I don't think I should open this. I don't even know who sent this. I'm not eating candy from someone I don't even know. There might be poison in it."

"Well if you aren't going to eat it, give it to me. I'll eat it."

"You've got to be kidding! This coming from the woman who would never even let me take a piece of gum from a stranger—how can you eat this."

"I'm old. I don't have anything to worry about now. I don't have to worry about you and drugs now—no one is out to harm you. Why would someone buy you a box of fine chocolates just to poison you? If some one was out to harm you, it would be easier to just run you down with a car."

"Mother!"

She stared at the woman before her. This was not like her mother. Something weird was going on here and she didn't have a clue what it was or why.

"If you're just going to just stand there, give me the candy. I'll open it." Her mother took the candy from her hand. "I'll eat the first piece. You'll see. There's nothing in the candy." She pulled at the clear wrap. "You know, maybe Harvey sent this over since he didn't send the rose."

"No. He would have sent a note."

"In that case, I wouldn't tell him about the candy."

She knew what her mother was going to say, but she asked anyway. "Why not?"

"He might get jealous. You know how these older men are. Insecure. He might think you have someone else after you...I'm serious. I know you don't think I know anything about men, but remember, I was once married myself. I know how they can be."

"Harvey isn't like that."

"All men are like that. Don't want any other bull around their herd. He's not going to like it."

"I'm not going to start a marriage keeping things from my husband."

"Ohhh—do you ever have a lot to learn."

Her mother bit into a piece of dark chocolate. Dark caramel strung from the piece of candy. "Oooh—oh—my," she mumbled as she brought her hand up to her mouth. She popped the remaining bite into her mouth. Chewing slowly, she commented, "That is so delicious." She licked her fingers. "See, there's nothing wrong with this candy. I didn't drop dead. Umm." She picked up the lid and read the identification of each piece and it's locations.

"You know in that movie, Forest Gump. He said his momma always said 'life was like a box of chocolates, you never know what you're going to get'. She must have never read the box lid. You always gotta read the box lid. Look, Godiva gives you a little brochure telling you which candy is which." Her fingers moved over the chocolates as she searched for her next piece. She decided on the one in the upper left-hand corner. "This one is cherry."

"You're just going to stand there and eat this candy not knowing where it came from or what the motive is behind sending it?"

"Yes." She replied, then turned and went upstairs with the box of candy in her right hand; her fingers of her left hovered over the candy, seeking her next piece.

Mary Ellen watched her mother climb the stairs. What was going to happen to her once I am out of the house? Since father's death, I have taken on most of the duties around here. I made sure all the bills are paid on time, the laundry done, the floor mopped, the food cooked. Those first weeks after daddy's death, it was the right thing to do. Momma was unable to do anything those first few days.

All her life, her mother—or so she seemed—was this strong woman, capable of handling anything life handed her. That was how she was raised, handling anything life offered. Yet when daddy passed, it was as if mother pulled her world as she knew it around her and just quit living. She never did anything, leaving all the chores, all the responsibilities of the household to her daughter.

Sure, if it suited her, she would fold the laundry, run the vacuum, but she didn't even cook her own meals any more. When father was alive, her mother rose early, cooked their breakfast as daddy got ready for work. His supper was on the table thirty minutes after he returned home from work. She managed their checkbook so accurately; there was never a bounced check, never a late payment on anything.

The house was always spotless, the laundry never piled up, and the flowerbeds always were in bloom. Spring flowers for spring, summer flowers for summer, even winter flowers for the winter. There would be flowers beneath the snow if the snow chose to fall on their home…and the pathway would be clean within one hour after the snow stopped falling.

Nothing was ever out of order. It wasn't allowed. Her mother knew how to fix a clogged sink or a leaky pipe. She knew how to do more then change a light bulb in her household. She was a woman of many skills and she believed it was all part of being the wife of the house.

But now? Now when I needed her the most—she had shut down. She watched her soaps, read her books, and walked in the sunshine when she felt like it. She went to church, but never to the grocery store, never to the mall. If she needed something she would just say, 'pick it up for me. No sense in me going out too'.

Mary Ellen ran her hand across her face. How is this woman going to survive once I am married?

She had mentioned it to Harvey, but his response had been 'she'll be ok'. She didn't really know what she wanted him to say. Mother moving in with them was not the answer. A couple needs to be alone to have that special privacy. They didn't need anyone living with them. She had never told anyone, but she was glad Harvey's children were grown. But still, her mother. Yet, she wanted to be alone with him.

Harvey. The candy? Oh, what was she going to do? Maybe her mother was right. Maybe there was no point in mentioning the candy to him. She didn't want him to think she was trying to make him jealous. Nor to think he had any reason to be jealous. No, it was best just to leave it alone. Maybe the candy and the rose were suppose to go to another Mary Ellen—maybe the names or addresses had gotten mixed up.

But she didn't believe that. There wasn't another Mary Ellen Forsman. Only one other Mary Ellen and she lived across town over on Lincoln Street. They went to the same church.

There were only two churches. A Baptist and a Church of Christ. Most people went to the Baptist. There was that small Methodist Church just outside the city limit, but even most county folks came to the First Baptist of Farley. Everyone knew everyone in Farley.

Farley, Alabama is a small southern town built on a square with a population of 1,879 at the last count. Cindy Miller was expecting twins in June. The town council was always glad when there were multi-births. Anything to stimulate town growth.

William Anderson founded the small farming community in 1814. He was on his way from Alabama to Texas, but his covered wagon hit a hole, broke an axle. When William and his son, Zack attempted to get the wheel out of the hole, the mule bolted, jerked the wagon, turning it over. The mules ran off and it was two days later before they finally found one of the mules. By then, William had decided this wouldn't be such a bad place to live.

Especially since he didn't have a wagon and didn't know if he would find his other mule. Besides, there was plenty of clear water in the stream that ran down from the hill. So, Farley was born.

The town was built around a high knoll. The streets created a square with the stores built on each side. William would not allow any newcomers to build anything on the knoll. Someday it would be the site for all government buildings, he informed everyone. His dream was to see Farley as a large town.

In the earlier years, the first jail was built on the knoll. Later a large sandstone courthouse was built in the middle of the knoll. The jail and sheriff's office was moved across the street from the courthouse. In later years the circle became a square, fashioned as so many small towns. The center of the town was the square. The knoll was where statues and monuments stood and public speeches held.

Politicians loved the knoll as they stood under the huge live oaks in the fresh air with their subjects standing below them on the grassy slope or in the street. It automatically lifted them up high and above everyone else, giving them an image of divinity as they shouted their vows of making Farley a better place for them, their children and their grandchildren. What voter could turn them down?

Yeah, Farley was small. William Anderson's dream of a large city would never materialize, but it was a place where crime was low. Farley was a good place to raise kids and enjoy summer evenings sitting on the front porch with the scent of wild honeysuckles filling the air.

Farley was not even on most maps and some people were glad. Don't let the outside world in on their sweet little secret...Farley was a nice place to live. Farley was safe while the rest of the world was going to hell. Everyone knew everyone and no one could wish harm on anyone in Farley.

The rose was for her—the candy was for her. She just didn't know from whom or why. She turned back to her lesson. A heavy sigh escaped her with the dread of lessons. Usually it was a pleasure, but not today. The rose and candy occupied her mind instead of students.

But she needed those students. They were her livelihood. They were what kept her from living off her mother. Her mother had money. Daddy's life insurance, his pension from the plant where he worked, and the savings they had accumulated all those years, plus the land they sold before he died. There were four rental houses he sold before his death. The money was invested. Her mother had money to live very comfortably, travel, buy whatever she wanted or needed. Instead, she saved all her money. She was too stingy to feed the birds in the park, and ate mystery candy that someone could have poisoned.

She sighed heavily. What a woman. A crazy old woman! Oh, God, why is all this happening now? These two weeks should be the happiest two weeks of my life. I should be planning last minute details of my wedding. Not worried about a yellow rose on the porch and mysterious candy at the door.

Chapter Three

She was in the kitchen when the doorbell buzzed. She glanced up at the clock. It was already six o'clock. It was Harvey. He was always on time. Not a minute early—nor late. She said six. He was here at six.

"Harvey," she beamed as she opened the door. He stood there in his dark suit, a newspaper folded under his arm. He had his hat in his hand. Most men his age did not wear a hat, but she noticed that about him at church. He always had his hat. "Come on in." She opened the door wide, welcoming her beloved into her house, into her arms.

He wrapped his arms around her, giving her a kiss on her lips. It was a light kiss, feather light. She knew it was because he was conscious of her mother's present. His kisses were warmer, more passionate when they were alone...when her mother wasn't lurking around.

"How is my bride to be?"

"Fine. Especially since I have you here." She smiled into his face. Today was Tuesday. One week from Saturday they would be man and wife. She dropped her head slightly. Oh she would be so glad!

"Did you have a nice day?"

She wanted to say no, but if she did then she would have to explain, and she didn't want to explain. She just wanted to put it all out of her mind. It was over and he was here and that was all that mattered. He was here.

"First tell me about your day. You know how things are around here. I did have four students today—usually there are six. Come on in. Here, let me have your hat." She placed the hat on the coat tree next to the door. "Come on in and sit down. Dinner is almost ready. The chicken should be out in a few minutes." She led him into the living room to the large dark green chair next to the fireplace. It was the most comfortable chair in the room. "Have a seat and tell me all about your day."

He sat down. She sat down on the ottoman next to the chair. This placed her lower then him and she looked up, an adoring smile upon her lips. He returned the smile, touched her hair gently.

"It was just another day. The paper seems to be growing and there is a need for more reporters. Farley is growing. More territory to cover. We are a newspaper whose respectability is growing beyond Farley. The county is counting on us to carry all the news and we must. That's what a newspaper does. Carries all the news." His hand stroked her hair. "Some of the older employees at the paper would rather we just stayed in Farley and the surrounding area of the county. But we can't do that. We must grow with the community. Even into other counties." He smiled, his voice drawing her to him.

He lowered his voice, almost as if he were sharing a secret with her. "I love you."

Her heart beat faster. "And I love you too." She too whispered. She didn't know why. They were getting married. Everyone knew that. The announcement had been in the paper, the church bulletin, and there had been three showers. One from their family, one from the church, and one from her students' mothers. She thought that one was the nicest one because she didn't expect them to do that.

Some of the ladies at church teased her about giving a lingerie shower but her mother had said that was foolish. That remark had hurt.

Not that she really wanted the shower...

Oh, yes she did! She wanted that shower just as much, if not more then the others. She wanted sexy lingerie more than a toaster.

She could feel herself beginning to blush. She rose. "I best check the chicken." Then she heard the bell. "There's the timer now." Quickly she left the room.

She was taking the chicken from the oven when she heard her mother. She didn't hear her come down stairs. Gladys stayed upstairs in her room all afternoon while the children were here—coming down only for a few minutes as she checked to see what the menu was for dinner. Then she had gone up the backstairs. But now she was in the living room with Harvey. She must have offered Harvey something because she heard him saying no thank you.

Oh, no! The candy! She was offering him candy!

Mary Ellen rushed from the kitchen. Her mother was standing next to Harvey, box of candy in her hand. Mary Ellen felt her hand go to her throat, her mouth fell open as a deep breath of air rush inward. What was her mother doing! Was she deliberately trying to destroy things with Harvey? Plant suspicion in his mind?

"Mother."

"Darling," her mother replied, giving her a bright smile. "I was just offering your Harvey a piece of these delicious chocolates."

"But dinner is ready. I'm sure he doesn't want to spoil his dinner."

"Oh, one piece won't spoil his dinner. Here, Harvey. Try this one here. It's a maple butter cream. I told Mary Ellen earlier that Forest Gumps' mother didn't know what she was talking about. She should have taught him to read the lid of the box." She laughed. Harvey laughed with her as he picked up the maple butter cream.

"Yes, she should have." He popped the piece of candy into his mouth. "Oh yes, very tasty."

"Dinner is ready." Mary Ellen wanted her mother to sit the candy down, forget about the candy. There was no way she could now explain the candy since she had told Harvey about her day, and not about the candy. He had not asked anything else about the rose. Maybe he won't. She stared at her mother, mentally telling her to put the candy down. As if her mother received her message, she placed the candy box on top of the piano as she moved away from Harvey.

The three of them sat around the dining room table. The bowls of vegetables sat on the table, the mushroom sauce was poured over the baked chicken. A basket of rolls set next to the vegetables. In the middle of the table was a flower arrangement of fresh daises, a pink candle was in the middle of the arrangement. Its flame gave a soft glow as it flickered. The china was pure white, the napkins a soft pink, the silverware their best. There was a tea glass and a water glass. The tea glasses were filled with ice, but the water glasses were ice cold and the water in them was ice cold. No ice—just pure cold water in cold glasses.

"Mary Ellen, you have set a very lovely table," Harvey commented her.

"Thank you, Harvey."

"She's my baby girl and she does a fine job at whatever she tackles." Gladys beamed.

Ok, everything was going good so far. "Harvey, would you like to say grace?"

They bowed their heads and Harvey said a short pray, thanking God for the food and blessing the hands that prepared the food. Harvey knew she had prepared the meal. She had not told him everything about her mother— the way she refused to help do anything since her father's death. She had a feeling Harvey just wouldn't approve nor understand.

That's when it hit her. She was keeping things from her husband to be. But there was just no need to burden him with these things, she assured herself.

Harvey finished the prayer and she handed him the chicken.

"I guess things are really popping down at the old newspaper, huh?" Gladys said.

"Well—I don't know if I would call it popping. There are always stories out there just waiting for us. The news is alive. Always changing, always happening. Stories come in all times of day or night."

"I could see that," Gladys said. "In my young days, before I ever got married, I kinda played around with the idea of being a reporter."

"You've got to be kidding?" Mary Ellen said.

"What? You don't think I wouldn't have made a good reporter? I know a good story when I see one. I read."

"No, mother, that's not what I meant. I just never heard you mention that before."

"I did have thoughts and a life before I met your father and had you. Of course, that was my true calling, being a wife and mother. No calling greater then a wife and mother." She took a bite of the chicken. "Good, Mary Ellen, very good. Have you two thought about children?"

"What?" Mary Ellen could feel her face blushing. She had blushed more since she had starting going with Harvey then any other time in her life. Why was her mother talking about children? She was thirty-four. Harvey might not want more children at this state of his life. He had four grandchildren!

"Have you two thought about children? I would like to have a grandbaby—at least one."

"Mother, I don't think this is the time or the place."

"Why not. We're all adults here. You ain't getting any younger. If you're going to have a baby, you need to make plans right away. Of course I was very young when I had you. Twenty-two, almost twenty-three. And if I'm honest, I would have had you even younger."

Harvey smiled. "But if you had her earlier, it wouldn't have been my Mary Ellen."

Gladys looked at him for a moment. "Oh, now I understand. For a moment there I thought you were saying if I had her earlier, she would have been older, perhaps married to someone else, your paths might not have crossed, or you…"

What on earth was she saying? "Mother, would you like some peas?" The question was purposed in the hope of changing the subject. But it didn't work.

"When I was a child, once I told my mother if she had

not had me, I would have still been born if that was God's plan. That my spirit was meant to be. She quickly set me straight and let me know if not for her, I would not have been. She could not understand I was viewing it all on a higher scale of the spirit and God. Now that I have my own child, I understand where my mother was coming from. We do like to believe we have a part in the creation of our own children.

"How many is it that you have, Harvey? Three? Four?"

"Three. Two boys and one girl. Gloria has two little twin boys and my sons each have a son."

"Oh, that's right. No little girls. Maybe you and Mary Ellen will have a little girl. That way Gloria will have a sister."

Sister? She doesn't need a sister! "Here, mother, have a roll." And please stop talking.

"Well, I don't really think Gloria would need a little sister. She's twenty-four. Jeffrey is twenty-nine and Brad is twenty-seven. I just don't think they would need another sibling at their age. I think Mary Ellen would agree with me on this."

"You haven't already talked about it. Will be married in two weeks and you haven't discussed children?" She seemed shocked.

"Mother, please. This is between Harvey and me. I don't think it's the subject for the dinner table."

"Hum." Gladys ate her peas and bit down on her roll. "Yeah, this is very good chicken." Mary Ellen felt herself begin to relax. Finally the subject was closed. She almost choked on her bite of chicken when her mother added. "I guess you can always play grandma to Harvey's grandchildren. That will give you some babies."

They ate the rest of their meal in silence.

Harvey helped her clear the table while her mother went in to the living room to watch TV. Harvey wiped as she washed.

They had washed most of the dishes in silence, making a little small talk about the pretty day, the early spring that it promised. As he placed the last plate in the drainer, Harvey said his sentences as if he was choosing his words very carefully.

"You know my age. I have raised my family. At this time in my life, I just don't really want nor see a need for more children in my life. I—well I know we haven't just sat down and discussed this matter, I—I just thought— assumed you knew. I don't want a baby."

"I guess I knew. Like you said, we never discussed it. I guess I never really thought that much about it. I—it would be a lie if I said I have never wanted children. When I was younger—the idea...

"I guess most women want children. That they think of getting married and raising a family. Of course, I'm...well...I don't guess most women would be thirty-four when they started a family. If I gave birth right now, I would be thirty-nine by the time the baby was ready for kindergarten. I would probably be the oldest mom there— at least the oldest first time mom." She smiled. "I guess some things in life just aren't meant to be."

"So you're ok with the idea of no children?"

"Sure." She didn't know why, but a sadness washed over her. She was sad for a child she would never have, never had truly thought about having, and was too old to have. Still, the finality of it made her sad. There never would be a baby.

When they went into the living room, her mother was watching an old re-run of *Friends*. She was sitting in the comfortable chair by the fireplace. That was the chair Mary Ellen wanted Harvey to sit in. She wished her mother would go upstairs and watch TV. The evening was a little too cool to sit on the porch. There was no place left to go but here with her mother.

Together they sat down on the couch. If he had sat in the chair, she could have sat on the ottoman again. It made her feel so close to him when they sat like that. He always stroked her hair while he talked to her. She would look up at him, smiling softly. It reminded her of an old black and white movie when love scenes were played out gently as the couple bonded together. The viewer could actually see the love growing between the characters. Not like today where they jumped into bed before they had even hardly kiss.

"Did you know all those characters are going to hell?" Gladys said.

"What?" Mary Ellen stared at her mother. Where does she get this stuff?

Her mother pointed to the TV screen. "Those characters. I don't mean the actors...I'm talking about the characters they are playing. See that one. He's bragging about how many times he's slept with a woman. They just sleep around and get drunk all the time. None of them goes to church."

"Mother! It's just a TV show! Those characters aren't really living beings. How can they go to hell?"

"You just mark my word. They're all headed straight for hell."

"But Mrs. Forsman, if you feel that strongly about it, why watch it in the first place?"

"Oh, I love that Joey. He's so cute! Beside, they're all good kids…just they're going to hell." She looked up at Harvey. "What about your kids, Harvey? Are they all good kids? I see Gloria at the market sometimes. She's nice. And at church too. But I never see that husband of hers with her."

"Ben. He's a good man. He works weekends. That's why he isn't able to go to church with her."

"Huh—needs to find him a job where he can go with her. Needs to be in church with his wife and those babies. That's something I can say about my Norbert. He was always in church. Good man." For a moment she glanced at the fireplace as if she was watching dancing flames. But the fireplace was black. There had not been a fire in ten years.

"And your boys. They live where? Denver?"

"Yes." Why was she asking him so many questions tonight? Usually he came in, she was polite, and after a few minutes, she would excuse herself so they could be along. She allowed him to court her daughter in a manner that was long passed. There were times he actually felt like he had stepped into the '50's as he paid his visits to his girl. Once he placed the ring upon her finger, Gladys seemed to approve and then she just faded into the background. But not tonight.

"Denver is where Mildred and I raised our family. I transferred here when the paper in Denver was laying off. It was just a small newspaper. We needed a change. Just felt like it was a time for a move. Ben and Gloria moved here about six months after we did. Gloria wanted to be with her mom after she learned about the cancer. They liked it here, so they stayed.

"Sometimes I think they stayed because of me. Just didn't want to leave me here alone."

"Now you're getting married." She got up, moved toward the piano. "I know they're happy that you won't be alone. Children—good children worry when their parents are alone—just like good parents worry about their children."

Is she throwing that at me since soon she would be alone? Mary Ellen wondered. But she said she wasn't worried about being alone. She didn't know what to think. One minute mother is happy I'm getting married and the next it's almost as if her mother was sabotaging the wedding.

"Mary Ellen, why don't you play for us? She has such a beautiful talent. She could have been a concert pianist if she had just pursued it. That would have been exciting. Don't you think so, Harvey?"

"I don't know if exciting would be the right word. I do know it would have also been a life of rejections unless you have the right break."

"You aren't saying she's not talented enough, are you?"

"Oh, no!" he exclaimed. "I know how talented she is. It's just some times in bigger cities things can be harder. More competition."

"And she couldn't have withstood such."

No, that wasn't what he meant. "No. I..."

"Well, I differ with you there. My baby girl can stand up to the pressure of any of them. Come on, baby, play us a nice little tune."

Her mother loved her dearly. She didn't doubt this at all. But she also knew her mother must have gone off the deep end as the wedding is drawing closer. She can not bear to be alone and she doesn't know how to handle it. She is acting out almost as if she herself were a small child.

Mary Ellen slowly rose from the couch and went to the piano. She sat down and finger touched the piano keys, running across them as she stroked the chords. "Is there anything in particular you want played?"

"Something soft, sweet melodies."

Her fingers touched the ivory keys and the sound of What I Did For Love filled the room. She knew it was one of her mother's favorites. Her grandmother played this tune when her mother was a young girl. Her musical talent came from her mother's mother. She believed that. Her mother thought so too, but that wasn't why she believed it. Grandmother Turner lived just outside the city limits. She went to the Methodist church. She played the piano every Sunday. She was eighty-one years old. She said playing the piano kept her fingers alive, loose, and her heart young.

And that she was. Young at heart. Nothing like her daughter. How could a mother and daughter be so different was beyond her. Oh, no. If that was true, then the woman sitting across the room from her would one day be her. She didn't want that. No way did she want that!

She kept playing. Maybe she would be like Grandmother Turner.

"Harvey," her mother was saying. "Would you like another piece of candy?"

She had not seen her mother remove the box from the piano. That was why she went to the piano in the first place, to get the candy.

Oh please, God, don't let her mention where the candy came from.

"This came today for Mary Ellen. She said she told you about the yellow rose. Did you notice it sitting on the buffet in the dining room? Marry Ellen, did you tell Harvey about this wonderful candy?"

Mary Ellen kept playing. Maybe is she played loud, Harvey wouldn't be able to hear what her mother was saying. But that wouldn't work; her mother would just talk louder.

"This is the best candy. Godiva. Not any of that cheap stuff. Here, have a piece. No...no...you don't want that piece," she informed him as he reached for a piece. "Here, have this one. It's dark chocolate with chocolate cream. Has almonds in it. I ate one of those earlier—very good."

"I don't care for a lot of heavy chocolate."

"Oh, really? Too bad. You'll like this one though. Dark chocolate is good for you. At our age we need all the help we can get to feel better."

"For heavens sakes, Mother, let the man choose whatever piece he wants!" Mary Ellen slammed the piano lid down.

"Mary Ellen!"

"Mary Ellen, please, darling," Harvey said as he rose from the couch. "Don't let yourself get upset." He pushed the box of chocolate away as he moved to his fiancée. "Darling. Are you ok?"

"I guess she's just nervous about the rose, and the candy since you didn't send them." She put one more piece of candy in her mouth, then closed the lid. "Good candy, though."

Harvey looked at Gladys, then back at Mary Ellen. He

had put his hands on his fiancée's shoulders to comfort her, but now he just stared at her. Silence hung in the room. The clock in the hallway ticked. The refrigerator hummed. The swing on the front porch squeaked as the wind gently moved it. But in the living room, all was quiet. Gladys waited. Mary Ellen stared at the floor.

Very low, very husky he asked, "Someone sent that box of candy to you?" She nodded her head. Never lifting her eyes from the floor. "Who?"

Silently she shook her head. "I...I don't know," she replied subduedly.

He dropped his hands from her shoulders. "Are you telling me someone is sending you candies and flowers two weeks before your wedding day and you don't know who it is?"

"Yes."

"I asked her too. She doesn't know who it is. Maybe it's some young whipper-snapper..."

Harvey turned around to face his future mother-in-law. "What are you saying? Do you know who it is?"

"No. Oh, no. ..no...no. I haven't a clue. I just thought about the idea of someone who maybe has this secret love for her all this time and now he knows if he doesn't act, it will be too late."

"Mother, will you please be quiet!"

"No, let her talk. Is there someone you haven't told me about? We've been dating for five months. You've had plenty of time to say something before now. In two weeks we walk down that aisle. If you're interested in someone else, you had better be speaking up now!"

"No, Harvey, no."

"Then why didn't you tell me about the candy?"

She wanted to say it was all her mother's fault. But if she did, it only made her look like some weak kid instead of being a grown woman. There was no explanation of why she didn't tell him. Other then, she just didn't.

"Look, Harvey, I'm sorry."

"Now, baby girl, you haven't done anything to feel sorry for. It's not your fault some young guy finds you attractive."

"Mother, please." Mary Ellen sighed heavily.

"Mrs. Forsman, I think Mary Ellen and I need to discuss this alone."

"Fine." She returned to the chair by the fireplace. She sat down, her back to the couple, her eyes gazing into the black fireplace.

"Mother, if you don't mind…"

"Oh. You want me to leave the room? Oh. I see." She rose from the chair, picked up the box of chocolates from the table by the couch. "I'll take these with me. I don't want them to be thrown at anyone."

"Mother, we aren't going to throw the chocolates—or anything else."

"Well, some time tempers can cause things to fly besides just words. I best take them with me."

Mary Ellen didn't reply. She watched her mother walk slowly out of the room, mumbling something under her breath about being forced out of her own house. Slowly she climbed the stairs. Harvey didn't say a word until he heard her bedroom door shut upstairs. At least she didn't slam the door, Mary Ellen thought.

"Now, you listen to me, young lady, there will be no secrets in our marriage. I want to know who sent that candy and that rose."

"I am telling you the truth. I don't know. Maybe they are just well wishes for my wedding."

"You believe that?"

No, but if she said that, then she would be right back where she started from. She never realized how hard it was to tell the truth.

"All I know is this, Harvey, I don't know who sent those things. I know we're getting married in two weeks because we love each other. No other reason. Right?"

"Well, I guess so…but I still don't like this idea of some stranger sending you things. What if someone is stalking you?"

"Harvey, this is Farley. No one stalks anyone in Farley. Everyone knows everyone. How are you going to stalk someone without everyone knowing who it is?"

"You don't know who sent that candy, and the rose, so you tell me?"

"All I know is I love you." She slipped her arms around his neck. Her lips touched his lightly. "That's all that matters to me—our love."

He returned her kiss. "Well…alright…but if anything else comes, I'd better know."

"You will. I don't think you have anything to worry about. Maybe it was just a silly joke."

He hugged her up close and kissed her again. She felt his hand brush across her breast, squeezing her breast slightly. She had never told him she wouldn't have sex before they were married. He just never mentioned. Maybe he knew she wanted that ring on her hand first. She wasn't so concerned about the sin, as her mother said, but what if something went wrong and here at thirty-four she found herself knocked-up.

She blushed.

"Why, baby, you're blushing."   Then she blushed again, the soft pink turning to sanguine. Harvey placed his hand on her face and kissed her passionately.

Chapter Four

This time it lay on the front step. Light frost was on the pale green tissue paper that held the rose. A white ribbon was tied around the paper. She found it lying there when she brought in the morning paper. She told herself she was looking for the paper when she opened the front door, not searching for another rose. She saw the rose before she saw the paper.

Mary Ellen reached down, picked up the paper, then quickly moved to the rose, knelt. Her eyes scanned the yard before she allowed herself to pick it up. There was no one in the yard. The paperboy would have had to see it. The frost was on the rose, but the newspaper lay in the middle of the porch, just like it did every morning.

Maybe the paperboy didn't see it, she reasoned. If he threw the paper from the sidewalk, he would not have necessarily seen the rose. She hoped he didn't. She didn't want anyone else to know about the roses. Her mother was enough to contend with.

Slowly she moved back inside. The paper held in one hand; the rose clutched to her side.

"Oh, I see you have another one," her mother said, standing on the bottom stair step. "So our mystery visitor returned. Still have no idea?"

"No." She took the rose into the kitchen, her mother close behind. She opened the cabinet door under the sink, and tossed the rose into the garbage. Then she went into the dining room and removed the other rose from the vase. It too went under the sink.

"What are you doing?"

"Throwing them away."

"But why. They're beautiful."

"And causing me all kinds of problems. I don't even know where they came from."

"Well don't just toss them away. I still say maybe it's your father."

"And I say if you believe that, you're nuts!" she blurted. She slammed the cabinet door shut, whirled around and left the kitchen.

Gladys pulled the roses from the trash can. She untied the white ribbon and sniffed the yellow roses. Sweet. Clean. Nothing smelled like roses. She threw the tissue paper in the garbage can and placed both roses into the bud vase. She placed the vase on the kitchen table. Then she went into the living room to Mary Ellen.

But she wasn't there. Gladys decided her daughter must have gone back upstairs to her bedroom, so she went up to her room. Mary Ellen wasn't there either. She went back downstairs. She looked around the living room again. Her books were lying on the piano. She moved into the room off the left of the foyer. This was supposed to be the study/library, but Norbert built just a few bookcases and collected very few books. There was a desk in the room, two chairs and a long settee that had belonged to his mother. There were blinds over the two front windows and dark blue drapes with tiny gold flowers covered the blinds. Most of the time the drapes were drawn since the room was rarely used.

She found Mary Ellen sitting behind her father's desk with her head down. When she was a little girl, she always wanted to sit at her father's desk. Her legs would dangle from the massive mahogany chair. It was in this room her husband played at the idea of being a writer. He wrote short stories, one or two manuscripts. He read the short stories to Mary Ellen when she was a child. He allowed no one to read the manuscripts, nor did he ever send them to anyone. They lay in a box in the closet along with all his short stories.

Gladys walked up to her. Mary Ellen didn't know she was in the room until she placed her hand on her daughter's shoulder.

"Are you ok, baby?"

"No."

"It's nothing to really be upset about. You know that, don't you?"

"No."

"Well, you should. Why don't you cancel your classes today? Take the day and just go somewhere. Just enjoy yourself."

That didn't sound like her mother. In all the years she had taught piano lessons, her mother had never encouraged her to cancel lessons.

Their eyes met. For a moment she saw a softness in her mother's eyes that she had not seen in years. Quickly it faded. Her mother turned away. "You need to get out for the day. Come on. Eat some breakfast…."

"No, I have a better idea. Take your father's car and

go for a ride. Stop somewhere and eat breakfast. It'll do you good. Get up now. Go call and cancel those lessons."

Her mother had never offered her the car for anything other then to run errands. She was surprised at the offer.

"Are you sure?"

"Yes. Now get up and go."

Thirty minutes later she was riding down Highway 33 leaving Farley behind her. It did feel good to be out of the house. But she couldn't leave it all behind her. The roses. Who was doing this? And why? There had to be a reason for it. There was always a reason for a person's actions.

But there were no answers. She pushed the questions away, freeing her mind as she sped down the highway.

She stopped at a small diner about thirty miles from Farley. She had crossed the county line and now she was in Dogwood County. The name of the diner was called Buzzard Stew. She smiled when she pulled into the parking lot. It was a small place, a green wooden building with a gravel parking lot. A big wooden sign hung down over the doorway. BUZZARD STEW. Home of fine vittles. Hanging on the window in red neon light was the word OPEN.

Mary Ellen opened the door. The diner floor held tables and chairs, and the wall was lined with booths; she moved toward one of the booths. A young waitress was right behind her, setting her flatware on the table as quickly as Mary Ellen sat down.

"May I tell you about our specials?" the young woman asked. Before Mary Ellen could replied, she continued. "We have country fried ham with one egg over easy on special. It's really good, and it's at good prices. $3.95. You can get two eggs for just $4.95. Hash browns and one biscuit come with it. It's a big piece of ham. There's even a small bowl of redeye gravy too."

"Sounds good. Bring me one egg, but scramble it, and two biscuits."

"Ok, but I'll have to charge you fifty cents extra for changes."

"That's fine."

"What would you like to drink?"

"Glass of water, small glass of orange juice, and black coffee."

"Ok. Have your order right away."

She left. Taking the menu with her. She returned shortly with the water and juice, and a small basket with jellies and butter. Ten minutes later she returned with a platter, which she sat in front of Mary Ellen. A large piece of ham covered half of the plate. Next to it was a serving of hash browns and her scrambled egg. Two biscuits lay on a small plate with a little bowl sitting in the middle of the small plate. Redeye gravy was in the diminutive bowl.

The girl left, returning quickly with a cup of steaming black coffee.

"Is there anything else you need?"

"No, this is fine. More than enough food. Thank you."

The waitress left again, leaving her ticket on the table.

Mary Ellen took her time eating her meal. The ham was good. A little salty, but good, the egg soft, the biscuit tender. Yeah, this was a good meal. This was the first time she had eaten breakfast out in—she couldn't even remember when. Her mother was right. This was a good idea.

Thirty minutes later she left the diner, headed north.

The highway would take her up into the mountains. When she was a little girl they went for rides on Sundays up into the mountains. Her father told her there were caves, waterfalls, and mountain lions deep in the woods. Her mother would never allow them to stop and explore the forest. A mountain lion was not going to eat her family, she always told them. Her daddy always laughed. Then she would laugh. They laughed as if they shared a special secret. But there was no secret. They just knew they weren't going to be a mountain lion's dinner. The idea was so ridiculous until it was funny.

She missed her daddy. She missed the life, as it was when she was a small child and he made everything ok. If the nights were stormy, he was there. If she was too scared to ride her bike, he held it until she was ready for him to let go. He was always there. Her mother was always there. They were safe with him.

Now she felt so lost and alone. Until she met Harvey. Harvey made her feel safe. Odd she had never thought about it before, but he did. He was strong. He knew where he was going, where he had been, and why he was where he was right now. She liked that.

She turned off unto a small gravel road. The rocks were like small pebbles—river rocks. That's what they were called. She once had an uncle whose drive was covered in river rocks. She wanted their drive covered in river rocks, but her mother said no. Her daddy said no, that her mother had the checkbook. Then he laughed. That was his excuse. He didn't write checks.

The gravel crunched under the car tires. The warm sun shone through the car windows. Such a pretty day.

There used to be a few shops on this road when she

was a kid. She didn't know if they were still open or not. Maybe they would be.

She drove for about three miles then she saw one of the shops. Mary Ellen parked the blue Ford, got out, locked the doors and walked upon the porch.

It looked just like it did when she was a kid. Rain and sun had weathered the wide boards, painting them a washed-out gray. A long porch covered the front of the building, and a rustic tin roof covered the top. High back rockers sat on the porch. Next to the door sat a round wooden barrel full of raw, light cream-colored peanuts. Metal pans hung on the side of the walls on large twenty-penny nails. A washboard hung over a large round metal tub that sat in a straight back chair.

She stood still for a moment, just taking in all that she saw before moving inside the shop.

A long counter covered one wall with a glass front and sliding wooden door in the back. Behind the counter on the wall was another cabinet, but this cabinet had no doors and the exposed shelves and pigeonholes filled with do-dads, and small figurines. The front of the counter was glass, where tall candy jars held orange slices, chocolate drop creams, peanut brittle, and fudge. At the end of the counter sitting on boxes, were moccasins. White, brown, and black.

A girl moved across the shop toward her.

"Can I help you?"

"Just looking around."

"Feel free. If you see anything you might be interested in, you just let me know."

Mary Ellen nodded her head. She walked through out the small shop, which turned out to be two small rooms.

In the second room, there were animals that had been mounted. Deer heads, a raccoon on a tree branch, and a red fox staring out into the space as if he were still listening for his enemy. Too bad he didn't know the enemy had already found him.

She walked up to the card stand in the middle of the room. There were pictures of sunsets, waterfalls, and caves. She wondered if they were taken in the forest. She picked four of them, the ones she thought were the prettiest. She didn't ask the girl if they were pictures taken in the forest; she wanted to believe they were. If she asked, she might find out they weren't. As long as she didn't know, then they were.

"Four dollars and thirty nine cents. You sure this is all you want?"

"Yes." The thought crossed her mind. Are they these mountains? But she turned around and left the store.

She drove further up into the mountains. She stopped at two other shops. They were very much like the first one. She didn't buy anything. Just looked around for a few minutes, then left. At the top of the mountain, she pulled off the road and parked next to some picnic tables. She didn't get out of the car, but sat there watching the sun go down. It had been a nice day.

Chapter Five

"Harvey called while you were gone."

"Did he say what he wanted?"

"Just said he wanted to check on you. How you were feeling. I told him you were doing fine. I know he wanted to ask where you were, but I didn't want to butt in so I just said you were out."

"Mother. You shouldn't have done that. You should have just told him where I was."

"What? That you wanted to get away. That you went for a drive. That you canceled your classes just so you could get away. How's that gonna sound? You saw how he was last night. You going to tell him about that last rose?"

She didn't answer. She didn't know what she was going to do. She guessed she would—didn't really want to, though. Didn't want to try to explain why she was getting roses when she herself didn't know.

"If you are, I guess you should tell him about the little box that came today."

"Little box?"

"It's in the front hall. Delivered by the same company. I guess you could call those people and find out who it is sending this stuff."

Mary Ellen had already left the room. She was in the front hall with the package. It was a small box, wrapped in brown paper. She looked at it. Then threw it to the floor. A loud crash filled the room. Whatever was in the package had been made of glass.

"Mary Ellen! What are you doing?" Gladys stood in the hallway. Tears were streaming down Mary Ellen's face. "Baby. Don't," Gladys said as she wrapped her arms around her. "Don't cry."

"I can't help it. Someone is trying to destroy me—my relationship with Harvey and I don't know why. There is no one who should be doing this. No one..." Her tears muffled as she cried into Gladys' shoulder.

"Don't look at it that way. Whoever is doing this must love you very much. They're trying to let you know before it's too late."

"Too LATE!" She jerked away from her mother. "Too late for what? I'm getting married. I have sat here in this house for twenty years waiting for someone to love me—but no one ever did."

"Baby, your daddy and I have always loved you and will even after death. Your daddy still loves you just as I will once I have gone home to my rewards." Gladys always spoke of her reward as *rewards*.

Mary Ellen turned away. "That's not what I mean, mother. I mean loved by a man." She glanced over her shoulder at her mother, then turned her back. Meekly her words fell from her lips. "Do you know what it feels like to listen to your friends talk about boys when you're fifteen—sixteen—talking about their dates the night before? And no boy asks you out. Never! Do you know what it feels like to sit at a party and all your girlfriends are laughing and dancing and you just sit?" She turned around and faced her mother. "Do you realize there were only two boys that ever walked upon our porch to visit me? Two. And neither one ever came back."

She sniffed. Her nose was running and tears flowing. With a broken spirit, she asked, "Mother, am I so ugly no one wanted me or do I just have a lousy personality?"

Her mother gathered her into her arms. "Neither. You are pretty, bright, talented, and very intelligent. Were you not an honor student in high school, the Dean's list in college? How can you say such horrible things about yourself? Any man would love to have you as his wife and be darn lucky to boot."

Mary Ellen looked up at her mother. In the midst of her tears, she laughed. "The love of a mother. What public office do you think I should run for to straighten out the world?"

Gladys patted her shoulders. "The White House, of course." She wiped Mary Ellen's tears with her fingertips. "Stop crying. Is Harvey coming over?"

"Yes. Last night he said he would be here around eight. He is going over to Gloria's for dinner tonight."

Gladys released Mary Ellen. "Wonder why he didn't invite you?"

Mary Ellen had wondered why. But she would not say that to her mother. The moment of confiding had passed. "I guess Gloria is pretty busy with the twins and just didn't want extra company tonight."

"What? One more person?" Gladys bent over and retrieved the box on the floor. She shook the box. "Glass. Whatever this was, you have broken it to pieces."

"Fine. If I could, I would throw it at the person."

Gladys tore the brown paper wrap away, exposing a small box.

James-Waterford fine crystal.
'It's as fragile, beautiful and sensitive to the
touch as his heart'.

"It was a crystal love flute, whatever that is."

"It's a vase."

"Oh, for the roses. Well at least, he's thoughtful."

"Mother! How can you say such? This nut is ruining my life!"

"Nonsense. Look at this way. Right now you are having more attention from men then you ever had in your life. You have one man wanting to marry you—another sending you gifts. What more could a woman want."

She turned toward the living room. "Are we going to have any dinner or should I just eat the candy?"

Mary Ellen gritted her teeth, shook her head, and rolled her eyes. "Mother," she said as she followed her into the living room. "Once I move out, who is going to cook for you? Do you realize you haven't cooked a meal since daddy died?"

"Why should I? Did I not wait on you and him all my years of marriage? I hung up my apron when I lost my husband."

"But you didn't die. You're still here and I just don't see how you're going to make it once I'm gone."

"I'll worry about that when it happens."

"It's going to happen, mother, it's going to happen. In twelve days it will happen. Then what are you going to do?

Eat your candy?"

"Maybe."

"Maybe? That's your answer?"

Her mother waited for a moment as if she was thinking. Then she said, "Yeah." She picked up the remote, turned on the TV, and sat down in the big chair. "What did you decide on for dinner?"

Mary Ellen looked at her mother. She could have remarried if she had wanted to. Her mother was an attractive woman. She had long shapely legs. Large hips, large bust, but she wasn't fat. She had an hourglass figure in her youth, but in her later years, the hourglass was still there, just bigger. She had soft chestnut hair, dark brown eyes that her daddy called cow eyes. In her youth, her mother was pretty. At fifty-nine, she was still pretty. So why did she stop her life?

Gladys looked at her daughter. "You never did say what was for dinner."

"Sandwiches."

At nine-thirty the phone rang.

"I hope I'm not calling too late," Harvey said softly into the phone.

Mary Ellen smiled. "No, Harvey, it's never too late for you to call." She was sitting in the living room on the couch. The phone was on a table at the end of the couch. She picked up the phone, moving it toward the dining room. She went past Gladys, who was still sitting in the comfortable chair. When she turned back toward the dining room, she walked behind her mother, and the long phone cord draped across Gladys' face and head.

"Hey, now, watch it!"

Mary Ellen didn't respond. She picked the cord up

off her mother's head and dropped it to the floor. The smile never left her face as she listened to Harvey talk. His voice was so soft, she could listen to him talk for hours without saying a word. His voice was so smoothing, comforting.

"Did I hear your mother in the background?"

"Um-uh. She's watching TV."

"She still condemning those characters to hell?" he chuckled.

Mary Ellen laughed softly into the phone. "No, she hasn't mentioned them anymore. I guess she thinks that's a hopeless cause."

"Are you talking about me?" Gladys called from the living room. "I can hear you if you are? You said she. If that she is me, then I want to know what you're saying."

Mary Ellen didn't answer.

Gladys raised her voice. "Answer me!"

"What is she yelling about now?"

"Nothing." Mary Ellen put her hand over the mouthpiece. "No, mother, we aren't talking about you." If she didn't lie, her mother would be in here demanding to know what they were talking about. "I guess it's the TV," she lied again.

Oh, her mother would say she was going to hell for lying, her brain moaned. Right now she just didn't care who thought what. She was lying to Harvey to keep him quiet about her mother; lying to her mother to keep her quiet about Harvey. In twelve days she would be married. Would there just be more lies, or would she finally just tell them to have at it.

She had never thought about Harvey having a problem with her mother. But then she also thought her mother liked Harvey. It's just now beginning to surface.

"And how was your day. Your mother said you went for a ride today. That you even canceled your classes. I must admit, that surprised me. I thought you never canceled those classes short of your death bed." He chuckled.

"Well," she began slowly. She had to say this just right. She didn't want him to think there was anyone else. Not after last night. "Normally I don't. I just felt like getting away for a few hours today. What with the wedding, the last minute details...it can all become kinda hectic."

"Yes, I guess so. When Mildred and I got married, we eloped. No fanfare. Just a quiet ceremony at the Justice of Peace's office. Quiet. Quick. Seems like more people go in for the fancy weddings now than they did back then."

Back then. Made it sound as if it was another lifetime. But then it was. It was his and Mildred's lifetime together. She really didn't want to think about his and Mildred's wedding when they were talking about her wedding day. This was hers. He was hers. Mildred was dead. Mildred was gone.

"Gloria had a large wedding. She and Ben went on a cruise for their honeymoon. They seemed to enjoy it. But then they should have since it didn't cost them one thin dime.

"Do you know how much a large wedding and a cruise can cost? Twenty-five thousand dollars! It was Mildred's idea. We actually took out a second mortgage on the house to finish paying for it. I didn't know it, but Mildred had been squirreling away money all those years to pay for our daughter's wedding." He laughed. "At first I was mad that she had not told me we had thirteen thousand dollars in a wedding bank account, but then thankful when the bills started rolling in. That Mildred was a planner. She started saving for that wedding by the time Gloria was a year old."

He didn't normally talk so much about Mildred. Or had she just not noticed it in the past. She wondered if he told Mildred not to keep things from him. Not that she wanted to. But then she didn't want to lie either, and she did just a few minutes ago.

"Tell me about your day."

"Nothing, much. Just the ride..." Should she tell him about the vase? Would it be easier if she told him in person? "When are you coming over?"

"Tomorrow evening, if that's ok. I'm just too tired tonight and it's late."

"That's fine."

"Is there something on your mind? Your voice sounds troubled."

"No. Yes. I mean. Yes, I do." No sense in lying. "I do have something I need to discuss with you."

"What?"

"Let's wait until I see you, then we can talk."

"What is it? I rather you just go ahead and tell me. Has your mother been giving you trouble again?"

Why did he go back to her mother? "No, it's has nothing to do with mother." She waited to see if her mother was going to yell out. She said nothing.

"Then what?"

"Today I received another package."

"Oh." His voice was somber.

"I don't know who is doing this. I haven't a clue of who would even want to do this."

"Could it be someone from church?"

"If it is, I don't know who."

"But it could be."

"Well, that's about the only place I go on a regular bases. But everyone there knows we're getting married."

"What about your students. Any single dads in the group?"

"No. Frances said something about her mom and dad getting a divorce, but I've never met her dad except at recitals. He seemed like a nice man. I can't picture him doing this."

"Serial killers can seem like nice men."

"Harvey!"

"It's true. What do you think they said about Ted Bundy? Nice man. You just never know what kind of nut this is. I think we need to call the police."

"Police? I don't know about that. What would I say? I'm getting yellow roses?"

"Roses? Did you get another rose as well?"

Oh, she had forgotten about the rose. "Yes, didn't I mention that too."

"No, you did not. Call the police. That's the only thing to do."

"I threw the rose away. The vase is broken."

"What happen? Did it come that way? That could have a special message to it if it came broken."

"No. I...I threw it against the floor and it shattered into a hundred pieces. Mother opened the box and it was a crystal vase."

"No marking on the package? No identification of the store it was bought at?"

"No."

"He's clever. Never leaving a trail to follow. Call the

police."

"But Harvey, I don't really want to bring the police into this. It will be all over town. They might even have it in the paper."

"You won't have to worry about the paper. I do have a few connections at the paper."

"I didn't mean that you didn't—it's just the police always give the paper stories. What if they give this one?"

"Like I said, I can handle that. Call them the first thing in the morning. Now you go to bed and get a good night's sleep."

She didn't want to go to bed. Chances of a good night's sleep would be slim. She didn't sleep well last night. Why should tonight be any different?

"Harvey, I'll talk it over with mother…"

"No. You are to do as I say. I am your future husband. Are you going to be discussing our business with your mother?"

"No, Harvey, but this does concern her too. The gifts are coming to her house."

"To you. Not to her. Call them the first thing in the morning. This subject is closed. You will call them."

His tone was firm—no room for second-guessing the decision. But it was his decision, not hers. She didn't want to call the police. And she was sure that mother would definitely not want to either.

"Good night. I'll see you tomorrow."

She responded with a soft good night. She didn't want to call the police. She didn't want to talk about Gloria or Mildred. Yet, she didn't want to hang up the phone. She wanted to talk to her fiancé about their wedding, about the excitement of their new life. Not serial killers and how great his first wife was.

For the first time she felt jealous of Mildred. She had never thought she felt jealous of her before. After all, the woman was dead. What was there to be jealous of? But now, as he talked about her, how smart she was, Mary Ellen wondered just what Mildred was really like. Did he love her more than he loved her?

Once she saw an old movie. It was an old black and white movie set in the thirties about a man whose wife had died, and he had remarried. He held his new bride on his knees, his face buried in her neck as he covered her with kisses. The new bride's face revealed the passion she felt as she tossed her head back, her long blonde hair falling backward. Then the man said those horrible words.

'I love you, but never will I love you as much as I did her'. The young bride's expression changed to pain as she leaped from his arms and ran from the room.

Would Harvey say those horrible words to her one day? In the heat of passion would he compare her inexperience to the wonder of Mildred? Would her cooking never measure up to Mildred's? Would their whole marriage be based on competition with Mildred?

The excitement vanished. In twelve days she would be married. Where was the excitement? Tonight she wanted sweet words whispered to her. Plans about their honeymoon discussed, not Gloria's.

She turned and went into the living room. All he could think about was who was sending her gifts. Maybe he should be sending her gifts? She was his bride in twelve days. Was he jealous, concerned, or suspicious? She couldn't tell.

"He wants me to call the police in the morning."

Gladys glanced up from her TV show. 48 Hours Mystery was on. She turned the TV sound down, but not off. She wanted to hear what they were saying, but she also wanted to hear what this crazy idea was that Harvey had come up with.

"The police, huh?"

"He said that it could be a serial killer." No, that wasn't what he said. He said some times serial killer were nice guys…no…known as nice guys. Dear, Lord, I can't think straight any more. Please help me.

"This ain't no serial killer. What makes him think of a serial killer?"

"No. That wasn't what he said."

"That's what you said."

"Would you please turn the TV off. We need to talk."

Gladys looked closely at her daughter. Mary Ellen was definitely upset. She clicked the off button. "Tell me what's going on. What did he say about a serial killer?"

"Nothing, but that some times a serial killer seems like a nice guy to people before they discover the man's true nature."

"Why did he mention a serial killer, and calling the police? I don't think that would be such a good idea."

"He's just concerned. He wants this person caught."

"Caught for what? Sending you nice gifts? That candy was the best I ever ate."

"Would you please forget about that lousy box of candy? It's not like you never ate chocolates before. You could buy your own box of candy!"

"Why buy what you get for free?"

"Mother. Can you not see this is wearing on my nerves? What if Harvey is right? What if this is some crazy nut, and he shows up at the wedding, and…"

"Like that movie, The Graduate. You remember that?"

"No! This is not like a movie! This is my life. I don't even know who this person is. This is a nut!"

"If you want to call the police, call the police. Do whatever you think is best."

"In the morning. The first thing." She turned away, but turned back and placed a light kiss on her mother's forehead. "Good night." Then she turned and went upstairs.

Gladys stared after her daughter. It had been years since Mary Ellen had kissed her good night. Usually they just said good night and each went to their own room. She touched her forehead. Why did she kiss her tonight? Maybe all this was hard on the child.

But why did Harvey bring up serial killers?

Chapter Six

Mary Ellen called the police at 8:15 after Harvey called at eight to remind her to make the call. Gladys did not think it was really necessary for him to call. It wasn't like they weren't capable of making decisions and carrying them through. They didn't need reminders. But still Mary Ellen seemed happy he called.

The police buzzed the bell at ten o'clock. Mary Ellen had been pacing the living room floor for the last hour before their arrival. Officer Nathan Oneal stood in the front hallway. In his hands was the yellow rose that Mary Ellen found on the step that morning. It was lying in the same spot as the one the day before.

"And you don't have any idea who is sending them?"

"No. If I did, I would march right over to them and put a stop to it."

"I wouldn't advise that Ms. Forsman. You never know what kind of person you are dealing with when it comes to something like this."

"I guess you're right. My fiancée told me that even a serial killer could appear as nice. You just never know what lies beneath the surface, do you."

"No, ma'am, you don't?"

"Ok, tell me just what are you going to do about this?" Gladys asked. She had been waiting for her soaps to come on, but right now, there seemed to be one in her front hallway. Cops, mystery gifts, jealous lovers—she was sure that's why Harvey had Mary Ellen call the cops—just jealous.

"There's not a lot we can do in a circumstance like this. We don't have any suspects."

"What about finger prints on the paper?" Gladys asked.

"I don't see how that could work. Paper is one of the hardest things to lift prints from. And you don't know how many people handled it besides the dropper."

Dropper. Well, so now he had a name. Dropper.

The most logical thing to do would be to stake out your house, but I don't have enough manpower to place an officer at your house. So we will check it as we make our rounds. Have you thought about watching your house and just see who it is? That would be the easiest way. Just make sure if you see the person, you don't do anything."

"If we aren't going to do anything, then why waste sleep?" Gladys asked.

"You don't want to put yourself in harms way."

"Hum," replied Gladys.

"What do you suggest, Officer?" Mary Ellen asked.

"Well, get a description of the person. Maybe you will know him. Either way, just don't approach him. Write down everything about the person. Then call us. We should be able to make an arrest then."

"Sounds easy enough."

"I guess you and Harvey could set up and watch," Gladys said.

"Harvey's got to work tomorrow," Mary Ellen replied.

"I can't ask him to sit up half the night hoping this person will show up to leave a rose. We have no idea what time he does this. It might be in the middle of the night or it could be five or six o'clock in the morning. I'm not able to ask him to do that."

"Why not? It was his bright idea to bring in the law. If you aren't going to heed to their suggestions, why did you call them?"

"Well, it is just a suggestion, ma'am. I have no way of knowing this will catch the dropper."

There was that word again.

"You do whatever you want. You will anyway. You want to stay up half the night, stay. Me? I'm going to be in bed. As long as all he is doing is leaving you roses, I see no harm."

"Oh, but that's just it, Mrs. Forsman. They start out with small gifts, maybe just watching the person and then they process."

"Process? What do you mean—process?"

"I'm saying you just never know about this kind of person. They usually get braver as they go along."

"Are you saying you think my daughter is in danger?"

"I am saying you never know about these kind of cases, and you have to approach them in a manner that anything is possible. And it is. You don't know their motive. You don't know who it is. They only thing you are really sure of is he comes in the middle of the night after you have gone to bed. The rose is there each morning.

"This delivery service. What do you know about them?"

"They're just locally owned here in town. Nothing unusual about them. They deliver things all over the county and even into the neighboring counties."

"I will check those for you. See if there is a lead there. Maybe someone will remember something about the guy who sent the gifts.

"How many gifts?"

"Only two. A vase. And a box of chocolates. I threw the vase away." She turned to her mother. She didn't have the heart to tell the officer her mother was deposing of the chocolates. There was nothing there that would help them.

"Well, I'll have this report turned in and see about having a car come by a few times tonight. Maybe the late shift can come by also."

"Thank you, Officer."

"Oneal. Officer Oneal. I'm glad to be of service. That's what our job is all about—serving the people."

Mary Ellen smiled slightly. Her mother stuck out her hand. "Well, we thank you for coming by Officer Oneal. If anything else happens, we'll let you know." She opened the front door. Murphy & Johnston's Delivery man was standing on the front steps.

"Oh, hello. I was just about to ring the doorbell. I have a package here for a Ms. Mary Ellen Forsman."

Officer Oneal quickly stepped onto the porch. "Let me see that. Who sent this?"

"I have no way of knowing. I just go in and pick up the packages I am to deliver. I never check to see who sends what."

Oneal inspected the brown wrapped box closely. Mary Ellen's name was typed on a white label. "Your company does wrap the packages, don't they?"

"No, sir. People bring in their packages just like they do at the post office. We just deliver. We're cheaper then the post office at Murphy & Johnston's," the delivery man gave his sales pitch. "Is there a problem here with our service?"

"No," Mary Ellen quickly answered. "There's no trouble here at all. Thank you for bringing the package."

"I need you to sign for it." Mary Ellen quickly scribbled her name across the white sheet of paper on the clipboard.

"If I go down to the main office will there be a record of who sent this?"

"No, not unless it's insured. Like I said, it's just like walking into a post office and mailing a package. We're just cheaper."

He stepped down the steps, headed for his truck. He stopped, turned back and said, "Are you sure you don't have some kind of problem?"

"No." Mary Ellen answered. She waited until the deliveryman was gone, then she said to Oneal, as she backed away from the box. "I'll let you open this one."

He inspected it carefully before removing the brown paper. It was a small box with a removable lid. Easily he lifted the lid. Inside was another box, covered in pick velvet. He opened it. A small heart shaped pin with ruby red stones lay on soft velvet. Officer Oneal offered the box to Mary Ellen. She quickly drew her hand back as if it were a scorpion.

"I don't want it," she whispered. She turned her back.

"Let me see," said Gladys. "Pretty. I don't know who this person is, but I like his taste."

"We know," Mary Ellen replied. "You love his chocolates."

Officer Oneal's bewildered look passed between the

mother and daughter.

"She's referring to the candy he sent. I loved them. She wouldn't eat them of course."

"You ate them?"   The officer could not hide his surprise.

"Yes. They were quiet good. Nothing wrong with them. I'm still standing here. Harvey even ate them too."

"Who's Harvey?"

"Her fiancée."

"Oh, he did? I am surprised you weren't concerned about poison. I would not advise you to eat anything else that might be sent."

"I truly don't believe this person wants to harm my daughter."

Mary Ellen went into the house.

"That's where you are wrong. Your daughter is very upset. He's already harming her."

"Her boyfriend doesn't help.   Talking about serial killers."

"Serial killers? Why would he think it was a serial killer?"

"I don't know. He just said something about serial killers."

"Serial killers don't work this way. It's probably someone with a crush on her. Doesn't want the boyfriend to know who he is. Her boyfriend—is he a big guy?"

"Just average. Why?"

"I just thought if he was a real big guy, then maybe this guy is scared to let your daughter know abut his feelings."

"Well he had better hurry it up. There's a wedding in eleven days. Eleven days. Yeah, he had better hurry it up."

When Mary Ellen came downstairs, her mother was

sitting at the kitchen table. Mary Ellen wondered why. It wasn't time for lunch. Her soaps were on, so what was she doing in here.

Mary Ellen opened the refrigerator and removed the orange juice pitcher. She poured a small glass of juice. "You want any juice, mom?"

Gladys shook her head. She had a writing pad in front of her, two pencils lying beside the pad, and an ink pen in her hand.

"What are you doing?"

"I am trying to think of how long Harvey and Mildred were here before she got sick."

"Why?"

"Because I just want to know."

"What difference does it make?"

"Maybe none. But can you remember? Had they been here very long before they started to Shady Grove? That's the first place I really remember seeing them. There wasn't anything in the paper about him joining the newspaper..."

"That's what they do with doctors and car salesmen. Not reporters."

"He's not a real reporter, is he?"

"Well...yeah...sure he is. He works for the newspaper. He reports."

"What? What does he report? The obituaries?"

"He does sports, mother, sports."

"Yeah, he does the school games too."

"What are you getting at? Why do you suddenly care how long he has been here?"

"And he said they were from Denver. I never heard Mildred say that much about where they came from. I heard her talk about the church they used to go to, but she never said that much about their friends there."

"Mother, what are you doing?"

"You know I have always been fond of Harvey, pleased with your upcoming marriage."

"But what?"

"No buts. I was just wondering about some things."

"Such as?"

"What make Harvey bring up serial killers last night?"

"I don't know—something about me saying Frances' dad seemed like a nice man, and he said serial killers appeared as nice. Why?"

"It just got me to thinking." She walked over to the counter and poured herself a cup of coffee, then sat back down. "It just seems like an odd comparison."

She sipped her coffee. "What do we really know about Harvey Broyhill?"

"I know I'm marrying him in eleven days. I know I'm in love with him. That's all I need to know."

"Mary Ellen, no wait. Listen to me. They moved here from a city we know nothing about."

"It was Denver, Mother, Denver."

"But how do we know that's where they came from? How do you know he has three children?"

"Gloria. Gloria speaks of her brothers. Has pictures of them in her house. He has pictures of his children and grandchildren in his house. I don't believe this." She stared up at the ceiling.

"What if he murdered his wife?"

"Oh, Mother, pleassseee."

She turned to leave the kitchen. She heard the phone ringing. She looked at the phone on the wall, but she didn't answer it. "I'll get it in the living room. It may be Harvey. I don't want him to hear your foolish talk."

"Well, it might not be so foolish if it turns out he poisoned his first wife."

She's crazy. That's all it was. Just crazy. When daddy died, mother went crazy. It was a slow process. That's why I didn't realize it. But the signs were there all along.

She picked up the phone. "Hello."

"Ms. Forsman, this is Officer Oneal. I just wanted you to know I went by the delivery office. They don't have records just like the man said. That's just a dead end there. The only chance is to way-lay him at night. Hoping you will catch him."

"Thank you for trying. Maybe he will appear again tonight." Her remark surprised her. She actually wanted the nut to leave her a rose tonight. "He's left one for the last two nights. Maybe he will tonight."

"If he does, you are not to approach him. Keep that in mind."

"Alright."

They said their good-byes. Mary Ellen stood staring at the phone when her mother came into the room.

"Was that Harvey?"

"No. It was the police officer."

"Oh, Officer Oneal. Nice man. Did you notice his mouth?"

Mary Ellen looked up at her mother. "His mouth? What was wrong with his mouth?"

"Nothing. He had a very pretty mouth. Most men don't. Does Harvey a pretty mouth?"

"I don't know. What kind of question is that?"

"You're going to marry the man and you haven't noticed his mouth." She walked past her daughter. "Hmmm."

"What's that supposed to mean?"

"What?"

"That little 'hmmm'."

"Nothing. Just thought it was odd you never paid any attention to his mouth. Like I said there's a lot of little details that no one has really paid attention to when it comes to Harvey."

"Maybe I was too busy kissing it!" she shouted as her mother went on into the living room. She followed her into the living room. "What are you trying to do?"

"I don't know what you mean."

"This business all of a sudden about wondering about Harvey."

"I just thought it strange his remark about a serial killer."

"He was concerned, mother. Concerned about me, your daughter. You should be glad he cares."

"Have you told him about tonight?"

"No, not yet."

"You going to ask him to stay with you as you wait on this person?"

"I just don't think it's fair to ask him. He has to work tomorrow."

"Maybe if you call him, he would be able to have the day off, or go in early. I just don't think you should set up alone waiting for a serial killer."

"What?" she cried. "Will you forget about a serial killer? What are you trying to do, scare me half to death? You're the one who ate his candy."

"And it was very good…"

"So you keep saying."

She walked away from her mother and went to the front door. The sun was shining brightly. A light breeze pushed the swing. She opened the door and walked outside. There was a bird singing in one of the trees. Spring would be arriving soon. The days warm and long, and she would be with Harvey every night in their home.

An odd feeling rushed over her. It would be their home. It wouldn't be Harvey's and Mildred's home with Mary Ellen moving in. No. She'd place her own handprints in that house and it would become their home.

She rubbed her arms. The breeze seemed cool all of a sudden. She went over to the large white wooden column, and wrapped her arms around it. Who was sending the roses and why? Four days ago all she could think about was her wedding day. Check on the last minute plans, going to showers, and selecting her honeymoon wardrobe. Now all she could think about was yellow roses and who was sending them.

She looked up and down the street. It was a quiet street, nice and wide with tall oaks that were old and strong. Why couldn't people be like trees? The older they got, the stronger they became, instead of becoming weak and frail in old age, their mind and eyes not as keen.

Harvey was fourteen years older then she. She had not truly thought about the age difference before. Not that he was that much older. There were plenty of couples with more than that between them, and they had long happy marriages. She knew if she was honest with herself—and who else could she admit her deepest feelings to—she really wanted his baby. She wanted the joy of holding a tiny baby in her arms after giving birth and knowing their love had created this joy. She wanted to feel the pleasure of watching her catch her finger and hold her tiny hand in hers.

She smiled. She had called her baby a girl.

But there would be no baby. Never.

She turned away from the column. She was too old to want a baby anyway. What sixteen-year-old wanted her friends to know she had an old woman for a mother? What eighteen-year-old would want a mother old enough to be her grandmother at her graduation? Harvey was right. She was too old. And he didn't want, nor need, another baby.

She sat down in the swing. She didn't notice the tears until the breeze touched her face, and cooled the warm tears that caressed her cheeks. She didn't wipe them, but the breeze dry them.

Chapter Seven

Harvey called her at 2:13 pm. She knew the exact time because she had just looked at the clock in the hallway wondering why he had not called. She thought he would have called earlier. In fact, she thought he would have called back even before the police got there just to make sure they were coming. But at least he was on the phone now. She needed to hear his voice—needed his strength—needed him.

"What did the police tell you?"

"Well, not a lot. Mostly that there wasn't anything they could do. The officer called back to let us know that he had gone by the delivery service, but they had no records for him to pursue."

"They've got to do something! That's what they're being paid for." She could hear the hostility in his voice.

"They suggest just waiting up for the person. Catch him in the act."

"What? That could be dangerous. You aren't really going to do that are you?"

That eliminated the idea of asking him for help.

"Yes." Her voice was steadier than her emotions. "I have no choice. This has to come to an end."

His voice heavy, his words loitered. "Are you—is your mother sitting up with you? I don't think you should do this alone."

She wanted him to say he would be there. That no way would he allow her to wait up on a—what? Was she being stalked? Was he an admirer? What was this person to her? Whatever he was—stalker, admirer, or serial killer—she knew she didn't want to wait on him alone. She wanted Harvey with her. Not her mother. She wanted the man she loved by her side. Protecting her. Her father would have. Shouldn't the man she is marrying want to be there with her?

"Mother said she wouldn't waste sleep over this. Officer Oneal said…"

"Who's Officer Oneal?"

"The police officer who came by. He said we should not approach the person on any account. So, mother saw no point in staying up. But I am."

She waited. Waiting for that moment he would say to her, 'and my darling, you will not be alone. I'll be there with you.' But she would not ask. She knew he did have work. But could he not take a few hours off? Be by her side?

"I would come over, but Gloria told me earlier this morning she wanted me to stay with the boys while she and Ben went out to dinner. I'm not sure what time they will return. And of course I'll need to be at the office early. But I will call and check on you. I was hoping I would have time to stop by for a few minutes before going to Gloria's."

She didn't say anything.

"You are alright with this, I hope."

And if she wasn't? Then what?

"No," she replied. "I mean...no, it's alright. Gloria needs you, and who knows, this person may not come. Just because he has the last two nights, doesn't mean he will tonight."

"I'll see you a few minutes before six. I'll be leaving here at five. Gloria asked if I would pick up the kids a treat since they were going out and the boys were staying home."

Treat? They could always have chocolates. She had plenty.

"They will like that," she replied. He said something else about the twins, but her mind was on tonight. He said good-bye twice, before she replied. "What? Oh, yes, good-bye, Harvey."

Again she was staring at the phone when her mother walked up behind her.

"You seemed troubled. Was that Harvey? What did he say? He going to rose watch with you tonight."

"No. He can't. I didn't ask any way. Like I said, he needs his rest. He has work tomorrow. He's coming by later."

She turned away and went to the piano. The pin was lying on top of the piano. She didn't say anything, nor did she look at it. She ignored it and the subject. She sat down at the piano and let her fingers stroke the keys lightly. The tune in her head came eagerly to her fingertips. But her mind kept carrying her back to the yellow rose lying on the front hall table. That was where the officer had laid it. She didn't bother to toss it out or to put it in water. The roses were poison.

They were creating poisonous thoughts in her mind. They were causing her to wonder about her future as Harvey's wife. Wondering just what role would she really play in his life. Causing her to think about babies that she never would have. Making her wonder why there never were any roses for her earlier in life. So many thoughts, yet no answers. Nothing but thoughts and that small tug of fear that was growing in her heart.

"Did you know I was watching this show last night on 48 Hours. It was about murder. This man murdered his wife. He buried her under this pond in his back yard. This little fishpond that he built after he murdered his wife. He told everyone his wife was missing, left him for another man. Would you believe they believed him, just because he was this real nice guy—a family man who went to church. They said he taught the youth."

Gladys stood behind her daughter. She did not respond, but kept playing her piano. Gladys moved to the side of Mary Ellen so she could look at her face and Mary Ellen could look up at her.

"It took them three years to catch him. Three years he taught the youth in church. Makes you wonder what he was teaching them. 'The sure way to keep your wife at home'?" She smirked.

Mary Ellen didn't say anything. "Then there was this other one. She was arrested for killing her husbands. The police said her twin helped her. It was a very interesting show."

Mary Ellen still didn't respond.

"Some times they have shows about serial killers."

She slammed her hands down on the keys. "I don't want to hear another word about killers—not another word!"

"Why? What's wrong?"

"I know what you're doing! I know!" She whirled around from the piano. "Don't think for one minute I don't know."

"I don't know what you're talking about. What did I say?"

"Killers. That's all you've talked about all day."

"I tell you what I saw on TV and you're upset?" Mary Ellen walked away. "Oh—oh I get it. It's not me. It's Harvey. Harvey's the one who brought up serial killers. Not me."

"And you're the one who started asking all kinds of questions about Harvey. You've known the man for over a year and now just before my wedding you begin to ask me foolish questions about him and his dead wife."

"I just wondered why they really moved here. Why this little town with a little newspaper. One newspaper. What if they didn't hire him? And none of his children followed him."

"You're forgetting about Gloria."

"Yeah, but only after her mother got sick." Mary Ellen walked back toward the dining room to the kitchen. "Don't get high and mighty with me young lady. Don't you walk away from me." Gladys followed her.

"Why? It's not as if you wouldn't follow me." She opened the cabinet, retrieved a glass and poured Pepsi into the glass. She got a handful of ice from the refrigerator. The Pepsi fizzed as she dropped the ice in the glass. With glass in hand she turned to face her mother. "I know what you are trying to do. And it won't work."

"What are you talking about?"

"You're trying to destroy my wedding. That's why you haven't been worried about me leaving. You don't want me to marry. You want me here, waiting on you hand and foot for the rest of your life. Well, missy, you can just give it up. It isn't going to happen. In eleven days I'm out of here. You're on your own. This house is yours to do with as you please. You can clean it, or you can let it corrode over. I don't care."

"How can you think that about me? Do you not think I want my only child happy? How can you think I would do anything to harm you?"

"You know, mom, maybe in your own sick way, you think you aren't doing a thing. But I know better." She walked past her. Then she stopped. She slowly turned around and stared at her mother. For a split second she stared, her eyes glaring into hers.

"You. You're the one leaving the roses. The candy. That why you weren't scared to eat the candy. It's you!"

"NO! No, Mary Ellen! No. It's not me. I promise. I swear on your father's grave, it isn't me!"

"Then you know who it is, don't you?"

Anger built inside of Gladys. First she was offended, then insulted, then mad.

"You listen to me, young lady! If I had something to say, I'd say it. I have for fifty years, and I'm not about to stop now. I asked you questions you should be asking yourself. Why did Harvey really come here? And why did his wife die shortly after they moved here. Cancer, huh? Well arsenic can be a slow death too."

She threw the words out there. They rushed into the

room like a cold north wind. Mary Ellen just stood there, taking the full force of their cold blow. Gladys turned her back to her daughter. Mary Ellen still did not move. Silence hung between them.

She didn't know when she left the room. She had stood with her back to Mary Ellen for several minutes. When she turned back, Mary Ellen's glass was sitting on the kitchen table, but Mary Ellen was not in the room. She wasn't in the living room. Nor the study. She went upstairs, but Mary Ellen wasn't in her room either.

Gladys went back down stairs. She stood in the foyer. She moved toward the living room, but she turned around, then turned back around, making a complete 360 degrees turn. She stood there, her hands resting on her hips. Maybe she had gone to the porch.

She wasn't on the porch. Gladys stepped down the concrete steps, her eyes searching the yard. She didn't see her anywhere.

"You looking for Mary Ellen?" Alice Petrie was leaning against the white fence that separated their yards, but Gladys didn't move toward the fence.

Alice was ten years older than her. A white headed, frail woman who thought she had all the answers to the world's problems just because she taught their Sunday school class. She didn't like being in her class, but there was no other class for her to go in unless she went into the younger women's class. And that would put her in Mary Ellen's class. She didn't think Mary Ellen would appreciate that.

"I said, were you looking for Mary Ellen? I saw her come out a few seconds ago."

She had to be careful how she answered this question.

If that old dingbat thought she and Mary Ellen were arguing, she would tell it all over Farley. She would probably have the pastor over here for counseling. She didn't want the pastor, and she didn't want Alice Petrie telling her anything.

"I saw her walking down the street. Then some car picked her up."

Car? What car? Oh, my sweet God in heaven, don't let the dropper kidnap my daughter!

"She spoke to the person very friendly. Seemed to know him quiet well. I couldn't see his face. They went that way." She pointed her finger to the left. "I don't think she saw me. I was knelt down in my flowerbed when she came out of the house. I'm sure she didn't see me or she would have spoken. Such a sweet girl. Always so friendly."

"Yes. She is." Who on earth would Mary Ellen get in a car with? Was it the dropper? Was he someone they knew all along and just didn't know it? Oh, don't let him hurt my baby!

"She seemed surprised to see the man."

"Huh?"

"The man she got in the car with. But I heard her laugh as she got in, saying something. Of course, I couldn't make out what she said. Not that I was trying. I'm not one to watch my neighbors coming and going."

"What kind of car?"

"Red."

"What kind?"

"Oh, I don't know—maybe a Ford—could have been a Chevrolet. I'm not good at models. It might have been a Honda. A little car—kinda, what do you call those little…aren't big enough for nothing. I don't remember the name. You see a lot of younger people driving them…"

"Sport car?" Mary Ellen got in a sport car?

"Sport car! Yes, that's the name. I heard my son, David, say he wanted a sport car."

You ninny. A sport car was a style. Not a make. This from Miss Know It All! She's stayed in that stupid hothouse of hers all the time until it has fried her brain.

Gladys walked on down the steps. Her eyes gazing south, the direction Alice had pointed. Who picked up her baby girl?

Alice was talking about her son, but Gladys turned and went back into the house. There was nothing she could do. She had to wait for Mary Ellen. She sat down in the big comfortable chair. Days Of Our Lives was on, but she didn't flip the TV set on. She stared at the black fireplace. She was scared.

Chapter Eight

"Mary Ellen Forsman! I haven't seen you in ages. Where have you been keeping yourself?"

"Right next door. I didn't know who you were at first. When did you get this car?"

"Last night. Picked it up at eight. I was on my way to see mom. She doesn't know I'm in town. But then I saw this beautiful lady walking down the street and, I just had to stop. That's just what this car needed. A beautiful lady riding in it."

Mary Ellen laughed. David Petrie had not changed since he was seven. He thought he was the cat's meow, Batman's cape, and Robin Hood's bow back then, and he still thought it. He was tops, in everything he touched. He was the important element.

A smooth laugh, a gentle voice, good looking. He was the quarterback of the football team, captain of the basketball team, lead actor in the senior play, class president, Beta club president, and editor of the newspaper and yearbook. His list of achievements had no end. His mother always brought over the paper every time his picture was in it for his achievements in high school and college.

They played together as children, but when he hit thirteen, he discovered a new role in life. Big man on campus. All the girls wanted him. He left her behind with their make-believe space ships in apple trees and stick horses. He was always the star; she was his sidekick. But he didn't need a sidekick when they reached junior high. He had a trail of followers, his pick of sidekicks.

She played the piano. He played football. She played the piano. He grew handsome. She played the piano. He began to date. She played the piano. He drifted away.

She looked at him. His sandy hair still had that gentle wave. His skin golden, even in winter.

He glanced at her, smiled. Perfect white teeth. And a nice smile. No, a pretty smile. Her mother was right. Some men have a petty smile. And of course, David would have a pretty smile. He would not have it any other way.

"What are you thinking?"

"You. Did you know you had every girl in high school at your beckon call? Yes, of course you did."

"Not you. You were always on that darn piano." He laughed.

"I had no choice. What was I to do? You broke my heart. You were my best friend and you grew up and left me."

"I didn't mean to, El," he said, calling her the same name he had called her all their life.

She was five years old when his family moved in next door. She watched the movers unload a bike, a swing set and she wanted it to be a girl that was moving in next door. She stood there watching, hoping. Then a car pulled up and out jumped this little white-haired boy. He ran around back. A golden Crocker Spaniel following him.

"Come on, Billy, come on!" he had shouted as they ran.

He never noticed her. She went back inside. Later when her daddy was outside talking to David's dad, she came back outside. She found out he was six. He was in the first grade. He gave her a smirk when he found out she was five and in kindergarten. But they became friends, best friends as they played together every afternoon in the back yard at her house or up on the Hill.

Until junior high. He went into the seventh grade, leaving her in grammar school. One year between them suddenly made a difference.

"I know." Then she laughed. "It was for the best. If not for you, I would have never learned to play that piano."

"And mother says very excellently. She said you give lessons to half of the kids in Farley. And that you're getting married next month…"

"Less then two weeks."

"Oooh…

"Mom says I should come home more often to keep up with all the news that takes place in Farley. She said I could work in Farley just as good as I can in Connecticut." He glanced at her again, grinning. "What do you think? Do you think I could work just as well here?"

"I think you should be asking your wife that?"

His smile faded. "I see my mother doesn't tell all the news. No, wait. Of course mom wouldn't tell that. Personal family business is kept personal. Carol left. Took the cat and left. After ten years she decided that life held more than a—how did it she put it—a would-be-writer." He gave a slight chuckle. "Or something to that effect. I'm surprised mom didn't tell you. It's been over two years.

"Would-be-writer? How could she say that? You had five books published."

"But not on the best seller list. No movies either."

"Yeah, but who knows."

He laughed. "You're something. Even when we were kids you always were saying you can do it, you can do it."

"No, I didn't."

"You don't remember that day you dared me to climb Mr. Barnhart's oak tree. You dared me to go to the top, the limb broke, and the fire department had to use the truck ladder to get me down. My old man whipped me. Did yours? No."

"My mother made me practice the darn piano, though." She grinned. Then she added, "I'm sorry about your marriage."

"Yeah, me too. But life goes on. It never stops."

"Your plans?"

"I have a new assignment next week. I leave for Africa."

"That should be fun."

"Maybe."

They drove in silence for a few minutes.

"Are you happy, El?"

"Happy? I never thought about it like that. I guess I am. Yeah, I'm happy. I'm getting married in a few days to a wonderful man. I wish you weren't leaving. You could come."

"Me too."

She leaned her head back against the seat. "Nice leather seats."

"Thanks. It's got a 423 motor."

Ok, she thought. She didn't know what all that meant

but she knew it was a nice ride, a very delightful ride.

They were gone for forty-five minutes and twenty three seconds. Mary Ellen knew this because her mother told her so just as soon as she walked through the door.

"I was ready to call the police. Don't you ever do something like that again! Do you hear me, young lady."

"Yes, ma'am, how can I not?"

"And don't you dare take that attitude with me. For all I knew the dropper had kidnapped you. Just wait until I tell Harvey how you scared me half to death." Not that Harvey would care.

"Don't you dare!" Mary Ellen bellowed out the words loudly. Her mother was shocked.

"And just why not. Oh, oh…oh, yes…now I get it. David. You don't want him to know you went joyriding with your old boyfriend."

"David was never my boyfriend."

"He was a boy and a friend. Boyfriend."

"Mother, don't do this. Harvey would not understand."

"What's there to understand?" Her mother dropped down into the easy chair. Picked up the remote. "What's for supper?"

Chapter Nine

Harvey came by just like he said he would. He arrived a little before six. Mary Ellen was in the kitchen frying pork chops. She only cooked two. One for her and one for her mother. Harvey wouldn't eat. She knew he would not change his plans. Her mother answered the bell.

"She's in the kitchen cooking supper. She said you had plans."

"Yes." He didn't slow down as he headed for the kitchen. No way was that old bat going to live with them. Crazy old bat! "Hi, darling," he greeted as he came through the door. He slipped his arm around her waist. She didn't turn around, but turned the chops. He kissed the back of her neck. "How was your day?"

She placed the lid back on the skillet, then turned to face him. He encircled her with his arms. She looked at his mouth. His lips were thin. She had never noticed before. He brought his lips to hers.

His kiss was warm. A tingle crept through her. She slipped her arms around his neck. She wished he would stay here tonight. Not go to Gloria's, but stay here. She wished they were already married and he had come home for dinner and later they would make mad passionate love in front of a roaring fire.

She pushed her body close to his, pulled her arms tighter around his neck. Then she did it. It surprised him. It surprised her. She pushed her tongue into his mouth. He pulled his mouth from hers. She let him go, dropped her head, and turned quickly back to her pork chops. She inspected them closely.

"Wow," he said, laughing nervously, "what was that all about?"

"Nothing." She did not look at him but forked the chops for their tenderness.

"You didn't tell me about you day." He touched her spine running his fingers up to her neck. She refused the excitement that wanted to run over her. "Was it a good day? Any more craziness going on?"

"No." Then she couldn't remember if she had told him about the ruby pin. She turned around, facing him, his arms around her. "There was another..."

"Mary Ellen, what are you going to do with this pin? If you don't want it, I do. I think it's pretty and no sense in destroying it like you did that love vase."

"Love vase?" Harvey let her go, stepping away from her. Mary Ellen stepped away from the stove.

"The crystal vase that came yesterday." She took the pin from her mother, giving it to Harvey. "This came today."

Harvey opened the box, stared at the pin. "You aren't keeping this. I can tell you that right now."

"That's just what I asked her. I am." Gladys reached for the box, but Harvey pulled it out of her reach.

"You will throw this away—out of this house."

"Now, here now—I want that," Gladys exclaimed.

"Mother, if Harvey thinks I should throw it out I agree with him."

"You would." Gladys left the room, shoving the swinging door between the dining room and kitchen. It swung two or three times before stopping.

Mary Ellen reached for the pin. "No," Harvey said, "I'll take it with me and throw it away for you. There's a dumpster at the end of the street behind that apartment house."

"There's no need in that. Here, give it to me. There's a trash can right here under the sink."

"And your mother will dig it out. I know her. No. I'll take care of this." He slipped it into his pocket. "I best get going. They're waiting for me. They don't go out that often."

"Alright."

"You be careful tonight. Are you still going to watch to see if he comes again?"

"Yes."

"I wish you wouldn't. I wish you would just let the police take care of this."

"There's nothing they can do...except watch the house. And we can do that."

"You be careful."

She stood on her toes and kissed him. He wasn't that much taller then her, but still she reached up to him. He smiled.

"You be a good girl. Don't let that mother of yours get to you. Soon we will be married and you won't be waiting on her nor having roses on your doorstep." He kissed the top of her head. "I'll call you in the morning."

She slipped her hand into his as they walked toward the front door. They had to pass through the living room. Gladys was standing by the front window, curtains in her hand, looking out the window. Mary Ellen wasn't about to ask her what she was looking at. She didn't want to know.

They made it almost to the front door before her mother spoke.

"Mary Ellen, what kind of car is that of David's. That little red sport car. Does it ride good?"

Harvey turned to Gladys. "Oh, you're good, Gladys. You're really good." A sarcastic smile touched his face.

"Why, Harvey, I don't know what you mean. What on earth are you talking about."

"Stop it, mother. You know what he means. The way you threw that little hint out there about David's car and me."

"So you went riding in David's car. What's the big deal? I'm sure if one of Harvey's old girlfriends came to town, you wouldn't mind if he went for a ride. Harvey doesn't mind you going for a ride with David." She turned back to the curtain, lifting it slightly again. "Such a sporty little thing. I just don't see how it could ride good though. 'Course, I guess it's the looks that matter."

She glanced back at the couple standing behind her. They had moved into the foyer. Harvey was clutching his hat in a tight fist. His face red, his mouth set in a firm snarl. He was saying something very low. Gladys couldn't hear what. Then they swiftly moved to the front porch.

She lifted the curtain again. She couldn't hear them, but she would bet dollars to donuts that they were arguing. Harvey had shoved his hat on his head. Mary Ellen had her hand on his arm. He said something, then turned and stomped down the steps. He didn't kiss her good by. Yeah, they were arguing. Wondered why? She smiled.

"Mother!" Mary Ellen shouted just as soon as she closed the door.

"What, dear?"

"Don't you 'what dear me'. You know exactly what you were doing and so do we."

"Why, I don't have the slightest idea what you are talking about."

"Oh, I guess it was just curiosity that made you ask about David's car just as Harvey was leaving. It doesn't matter what you do," she said as she stalked away. "I am getting married in ten days. And there nothing you can do about it."

"Eleven days, dear. And whoever said I didn't want you to get married. My goodness, you're old enough to make your own decision concerning marriage. I would never stand in your way."

"You can rattle on all you want to. You will not deter us from this marriage." She walked into the kitchen. In a few seconds she stuck her head back into the dining room. "Oh, thanks to your little remark about the car, I forgot about the pork chops. They're burned."

"Oh, now I see how it's going to be. Every time you and Harvey have a little spat, you're planning on laying the blame at my feet. It's not my fault the man you are marrying is a hot head."

Mary Ellen slammed the door. It swung back and forth. Gladys stood there watching the door until it stopped. Then she sat down in the comfortable chair and flipped the remote.

Mary Ellen sat the burned chops on the table with the creamed potatoes and lima beans. The rolls she was planning on cooking, but forgot after Harvey came, were still sitting on the counter. She thought about sitting them on the table too, but decided it would do no good. Knowing her mother she would eat them raw and then complain about stomach problems from the lousy meal The only thing she could do was serve a few pieces of white bread.

She reached up into the cabinet and removed a loaf of white bread. She laid three slices on a small plate.

"Mother," she called without leaving the kitchen. "Dinner is ready." She should have said served. Playing the role of the servant. For a moment she thought about taking her mother's plate to the dining room table, placing it there with her tea and then she, the help, would eat in the kitchen. Before she could remove the plate from the table, her mother came through the kitchen door.

"How bad did you burn the chops?" Mary Ellen pointed at them. "Well, I guess I can peel off the burned brown. 'Course that is the best part. That's the best part of fried chicken too—the brown—the crunches—if it ain't burned." She pulled out her chair and sat down. Mary Ellen stood by the stove. "You going to sit down?"

Mary Ellen slowly pulled out her chair. She thought about not eating, but she was hungry. And she did cook it.

"Pass me those limas," Gladys said as she placed a chop on her plate. She handed the platter to Mary Ellen with one hand, took the lima beans with the other. "I want those potatoes also."

Spoons were clicking the sides of the bowls as Gladys dipped her food, then sat the bowls on the table. She picked up a piece of bread. Then she spotted the rolls sitting on the counter.

"You forget your rolls? Rolls sure would have been better than this white bread. Course don't guess it really makes any different." She cut her pork chop. As she forked a piece of meat, she said, "I don't think Harvey should have taken that little heart pin."

"He's going to throw it away for me. The same thing I should have been doing with all that junk, including your candy."

"No, not the candy now." She ate her chop. Mary Ellen put her food on her plate. "Well, I don't think he should have taken the pin. What if the police wants to see it?"

Then she dropped her fork onto her plate. It was as if a light bulb had gone off in her brain. If she were a cartoon figure, there would have been one above her head. Mary Ellen did not like the expression on her mother's face.

"Why didn't they check it for prints? They always check for prints on TV. So why didn't these cops?" She slammed the table with the palms of her hands. "They don't believe us! That's the only logical reason why they would not have taken it with them."

"I don't know about that, Mother. The officer seemed eager to help. He did go to the delivery company."

"Or so he says. Remember what Harvey told you, even serial killers could seem like nice people. You've got to learn that, Mary Ellen. Just because someone smiles at you in a friendly way, doesn't mean they're nice. Remember that."

She pushed back her chair. "I'm going to call that cop. He's got some questions to answer, and he'd better have the right answers."

"Mother, please, don't make things worse. He might not help at all if he thinks we don't believe anything he is telling us."

"I'm calling. You can't talk me out of this."

Tell me something I don't already know, Mary Ellen

thought.

Gladys picked up the phone receiver off the wall. She made a quick dial. "I want to speak to Officer Nathan Oneal."

She waited a few seconds. "Then where can I reach him. Where does he live? What do you mean you can't tell me? Don't you know where he lives? He is a cop, isn't he? Can't you keep up with where your own officers live?"

Again she was silent. "I don't care if that is your policy. This is important. Maybe life or death. You get a hold of that man, and you tell him to call me. Gladys Forsman." Again silence from Gladys. "Who am I? Your boss!"

Mary Ellen dropped her head into her hands as her mother gave the officer her telephone number. Gladys hung up the phone. She turned to face Mary Ellen.

"What?"

Mary Ellen raised her head. "Nothing. Not a thing."

"You get on that phone and call Harvey. You tell him you want that pin back. They can check it for prints."

"But, Mother…"

"Call him. Has he got a cell phone? Got to get ahold of him before he throws it away."

"He already has. He was going to throw it in the dumpster as the end of the street."

Gladys sat down in her chair again. "Ok." She finished her dinner, then got up from the table. She didn't say where she was going. She went to the front hall, removed her sweater from the coat tree, and went out the front door.

Mary Ellen finished her dinner in peace.

Chapter Ten

She knew a dumpster stank, but she didn't realize just how bad until she pulled up the lid and stuck her head over into it.

"Whew!" She snarled her nose. Her flashlight gave a small round beam of light into the dumpster. Now if that man had just given her the pin when she asked, he would have saved her a lot of trouble. She threw the lid backward. It hit the back of the dumpster with a loud bang. Gladys looked around. There were security lights at each end of the apartment complex. Maybe no one was outside their apartment to hear the noise. She didn't see anyone.

That's the last thing she needed—some nosey snob coming over here and asking just what did she think she was doing.

She moved a piece of newspaper, tossed an old baby car seat aside. The beam from her flashlight swept across black plastic garbage bags, and one or two pink ones. But she didn't see the little pink box. With her luck it fell all the way to the bottom.

She glanced over her shoulder. Still no one in sight. She lifted the second section of the dumpster's lid. Now it was fully opened. Again she glanced around. She was nervous, but there's no need to be, she told herself. There's no one out here but her. And no one cared if she was in a dumpster.

She placed her left foot on a metal slot that was used

by the garbage truck to pick up the dumpster. With one foot in the slot, Gladys boosted herself upward.

Not bad for an old woman. Maybe she should have been a private eye...kinda like *Kinsey Millhone* in *Sue Grafton's* mystery novels.

She threw her right foot over into the dumpster, setting it on one of the garbage bags. As she lifted her left foot, the bag she had placed her right foot on slipped, and she fell in. Another bag tumbled and the car seat fell toward her, hitting her on the head. She slipped further into the dumpster, the flashlight falling from her hand.

"Darn!" She rubbed her head. The beam of light shined back up to her from the far corner. She stood up, carefully moving toward the flashlight.

Picking it up, she flashed the light about. How was she going to find that pin in all this mess? That little box probably fell to the bottom—unless—maybe—just maybe it got caught on top of a bag. She doubted if there had been any bags placed in here since Harvey threw the pin away. There wasn't time.

Ok, now lets see, she said to herself, as she attempted to get her bearing if he tossed the pin in, it could have fallen straight down. That would put it in front of the door. But there's two sliding doors on this thing—and if he threw it—(he was mad)—it could be at the back—or bounced off the metal sides. In other words, it could be anywhere in this stinking place.

Slowly she moved the light over each bag. Satisfied the pin wasn't on top of any of the bags, she began to push them aside, working downward. She tossed the bags with one hand, the other searching with the light. Still nothing—nothing she would want to take home with her anyway. Just a lot of smelly garbage bags…all colors.

She never realized garbage bags came in so many colors. Things had really perked up at the grocery store. Colored garbage bags…

She leaned over closer to one of the blue ones. Scented to boot. Maybe she should go the grocery store and see what else was new in the last ten years.

She threw the blue bag over her shoulder toward the back of the dumpster. It hit the side of the dumpster, then rolled back down, hitting the back of her leg, causing her to fall backward. She landed on a pile of soft garbage bags. Then she heard it.

A loud high pitched sound filled the dumpster. Gladys jumped up! Plastic bags were clawed, paper rattling. She quickly shone the light in the direction of the noise. The noise stopped. Small eyes stared into the light, and thin long whiskers flicked.

She screamed. It ran. A long skinny hairless tail flicked the side of a plastic bag in the rat's hasty departure. Gladys screamed again—her voice filling the air, her body shaking, her arms waving. Backing up, she bumped into another bag that rolled downward and landed on top of her foot.

Quickly she threw the beam of light on the bag of garbage. A small round head poked out of a hole in the bag, glaring at her. As if the light blinded it, the rat stared into the golden beam, motionless except for a twitching nose. Gladys kicked her foot upward, sending bag and beast into the air.

She scrambled for the dumpster's side, trying to get out of her hole of garbage and rats. She grabbed the side of the dumpster, trying to hoist up her leg without stepping on more bags. But she had no choice. She had to use the bags as leverage to get out. She climbed atop a pile of plastic bags, then finally, she jostled her body upward onto the edge of the dumpster, threw one leg over, pushing her body across the dumpster's edge until she straddled the dumpster's side.

"May I help you?"

She looked down. A young police officer in his dark blue uniform stood beside the dumpster.

"You sure can. Here, give me a hand." Gladys leaned forward, practically falling into the officer's arms. "I sure am glad you came along. What took you so long?" She felt strong and brave now that she was once again standing on steady ground and not floundering on garbage bags.

"Ma'am?"

"I thought I was never going to get out of there. What took you so long? Don't you think you could have gotten here a little quicker."

"And what were you doing in there and why would you think I was coming?"

"You are here to serve and protect, are you not?"

"Well, yes."

"Then why wouldn't I think you would be here." Gladys began to knock off some of the debris from her sweater. "Now if you will excuse me, I will be going."

"Oh, no. Not so fast." The officer held his flashlight high, shining it into Gladys' face. She in turn shined her light into his. He blinked. "If you don't mind..." He dropped his light away from her face, letting it sweep across her body. Gladys moved her light over his body, then letting it rest on his badge. She also noticed his name on the right side of his shirt.

"Walker, huh." Then she smiled. "Any kin to *Ranger Walker?*"

"What were you doing in that dumpster?"

"Did I break the law by being in there?"

"I ask the questions. What were you doing in the dumpster?" Gladys tilted her head, looking directly into Officer Walker's eyes. "I'm waiting."

"I don't really have to answer your questions, do I?"

"Why wouldn't you want to answer my questions? What do you have to hide?"

"I never said I had anything to hide. I just don't have to answer your questions if I don't want to, now do I?" Her mouth set firmly. She was not about to tell him what she was doing in that dumpster. In the first place, it wasn't any of his business. This was a free country. She was over twenty-one. She didn't have to report to anyone why she was in a dumpster. There were no laws about being in a dumpster…or at least she didn't think there were. She sure hoped there wasn't!

"I can also take you down to the station for a few questions if that's what you want."

Gladys could feel her blood rising. "And just why would you do that?" she demanded.

"You are either a vagrant, or you're in private property without permission."

"How do you know the manger of the apartment house didn't give me permission?"

"I don't have to ask him. This isn't his dumpster. Did you call Land's Sanitation Service?" Gladys didn't reply. "I didn't think so. Now, one last time, what were you doing in the dumpster?"

One last time, huh? Well, he just didn't know who

he's dealing with. A little ride down town wasn't going to scare her. If she wanted to climb into a dumpster, that was her business—not his!

She clammed up. She closed her mouth tightly, set her jaw, and crossed her arms. Officer Walker shook his head, then caught hold of her arm. "Come with me. I'm not going to cuff you if you come peacefully. You can decide just what you are going to do when we get to the station."

"Yeah, there's plenty I'll have to say to your superior. The very idea that you would arrest an old woman just because she is in a dumpster!"

"I don't care who you know! I'm not calling Sergeant Oneal. This is his night off. There's nothing here we can't handled without him. Now, what's your name?"

Gladys stood before the night shift sergeant's desk. He sat behind his desk in his dark blue uniform, pencil in hand. He glared at Gladys. "Ok, lady, if you don't give me your name, I'm going to charge you with trespassing, resisting arrest, destroying private property. And I don't know what else."

"I wasn't trespassing, I didn't resist arrest, and I sure as heck didn't destroy any property. I was in a dumpster!"

"And why were you in a dumpster?"

She gave him a long hard stare. On his uniform was the name Nash. On his sleeve were sergeant stripes.

He was a small man with thick dark brown hair. It could have been a pretty color, but it wasn't. It was slicked down with oil. His eyebrows were dark and brushy but they were also flaky. Little white flakes were scattered throughout the brows. You didn't have to look closely to see them. It was almost as if they were resting on each hair. It gave his brows a dry scaly appearance. There was also a crusty patch between his eyes.

He was clean—or at least he didn't smell, Gladys decided. He just didn't look clean. She didn't like him. Didn't like his tone. His looks. Nothing about him.

"I want to speak with Officer Oneal," she demanded.

"I told you. He's off duty. Anything you can tell him, you can tell us." He gave Gladys a once over from head to toe. Smelly, dirty, hair askew. Probably homeless, looking for food—although she didn't look undernourished. There was a red mark on her forehead. Maybe they should just commit her overnight to the hospital. Wonder what her state of mind is. She seemed a little flakey.

Gladys took one step backward. She didn't like the way he was looking at her. Like she was some kind of criminal.

"Gladys! What are you doing here?"

Gladys turned. Tony Lambright was walking toward her. Oh darn! She had forget about the pastor's son being a cop. He had just finished training about four weeks ago. Alice had mentioned it in their Sunday School Class. Now what was she going to do?

The desk sergeant turned his head toward Tony. "You know this—this woman." He almost said nut. "What's her name?"

"Name?" Tony stood in front of Gladys now, holding a Styrofoam cup of hot streaming coffee. He looked at Gladys. For some reason he got the feeling that Gladys didn't want him to know her. But he had no choice. He had a duty to his badge. Besides, he had already called her by name.

"Gladys," he touched her elbow, guiding her away from the others. "What's going on here?"

Gladys' eyes darted back to the sergeant. "It's those cops. They picked me up for no good reason. They won't let me speak to my officer."

"Your what?"

"Don't I get to make one phone call?"

"Well yeah, if you're arrested...what's going on here?"

"You just tell them I want to make my phone call and if they aren't going to do that, then they best just go ahead and throw me into the slammer."

"No one is throwing you into the slammer."

"That's what they've got in mind. They won't call my officer."

"Your officer? What are you talking about? Officer? You mean lawyer? I don't see why you would need a lawyer. Why don't you just answer their questions? What are you doing here?"

"It's a long story, Tony. Just make them let me make my phone call. Then we'll get everything straightened out."

"Let me see..." He walked over to the other two officers. Gladys stood back, watching. Tony said something, then he turned back to Gladys. He motioned for her to come to him. "They said ok. Just make it from Sergeant's desk phone."

Gladys glazed at the two again. She didn't know about that. "Ok, but you guys step away from the desk. This is a private call."

The three officers moved away from the desk, keeping Gladys in view.

"You got a phone book?"

The three glanced at one another. Phone book? Didn't she know her own number?

"Yeah," Sergeant said. "Left hand corner."

Gladys pulled open the drawer, removed the book. Finding the number she wanted, she dialed the phone number. She waited. On the third ring, it was answered.

"Hello."

"I need you to get down here right now. Where am I? The police station. They're trying to arrest me. No. They don't have any grounds. They are trying to drum up all these bogus charges.

She listened for a moment. "No. No. That won't do. I want you here. They don't even know what they're doing. How long? Ten minutes. Ok. I'm waiting."

She replaced the receiver. Then moved over to a chair against the wall to the left of the sergeant's desk.

"Tony," Officer Walker said, "just who is that woman?"

Tony Lambright looked at the woman sitting in the chair against the wall. Gladys Forsman never looked like this! Where had she been? What was she doing here? And what was his daddy going to say when he found out one of his parishioners was in trouble with the law. He smiled. It really was kinda funny. Then he remembered the two officers standing beside him. His supervisor waited.

"She goes to my church."

"You're kidding!" Officer Walker said.

"I hope she comes a little cleaner than she is now. And smells a little better," Sergeant Nash said. The old bat! He hated dealing with these jerks that came in here thinking they own the department, yelling he worked for them because they were taxpayers. Some nut told him just tonight, she was his boss. He cut his eyes toward Gladys.

Come to think of it...that voice on that phone sounded just a little like this old bat.

He went back to his desk and pulled a file that was lying on the in-box on his desk. This box held the files of cases he received calls on. He sat down and scanned the file.

Gladys Forsman.

"Mrs. Forsman." A smiled touched his mouth. It gave him great pleasure to call her by her name. Police work in action. He was a natural born detective. And some of his peers thought he would never make a good cop because he was fat. Fat has nothing to do with a cunning mind.

Her eyes roamed over the office like an eagle, probing out its snare, waiting for its escape. Surprised, she heard her name called. Gladys glared at him.

"I see here where you called earlier."

She didn't give her number. So the big city of Farley' police station has caller ID. Was that not a violation of her privacy? She would make a note of that. Or did Tony talk. She'd make a note of that too.

Nathan Oneal shoved open the door. He stared at Gladys with a long hard stare. Just what was this woman trying to do?

"Mrs. Forsman," he greeted as he walked over to her. "Now would you tell me just what is going on here? I called your house. Your daughter said she didn't know where you went. She seemed worried. And then, I get a call from you. You tell the police it is a matter of life and death, and then you tell me the police are after you." He stood back. His eyes traveled over Gladys.

"Where have you been?" Gladys rose, started toward him. He held up his hands. "Please, that's close enough. I do believe I know where you've been, I just want to know why. You smell like you have been in a garbage pile."

"And you would be just about right." The desk sergeant told Oneal. "What are you doing here?" He stopped. "Oh wait. Let me guess. This was your phone call. How did you get his number?"

Gladys smiled. She wasn't going to tell him she got it off the file-wheel as she got the book from the desk drawer. A person can do a lot when the back is turned. She knew a few tricks.

"Can you not handle her complaint? What's this business about her being arrested?" Oneal asked.

"No one has arrested her. We—or rather Officer Walker found her climbing out of a dumpster. She wouldn't tell what she was doing or who she was. So he brought her in."

"Why didn't you just let her go?" Oneal asked Walker. "What could she have been after in a dumpster? If it was food, maybe you should have just fed her and saved the taxpayers of Farley a little money. This is a waste of time." He turned to Gladys. "Mrs. Forsman, were you looking for food?" he asked sarcastically.

"No." Her voice just as sarcastically. Gladys motioned for Oneal to come a little closer. Oneal scoffed. "I'm not contagious." She waited.

"I can hear you. What is it?"

"We need to talk privately."

"Come on." He took her across the room to his desk. "Ok, what is it and this had better be good. What were you doing in that dumpster?"

"This is your fault."

"My fault!", he exclaimed. Then he quickly glanced

around, making sure no one heard him. "You want to tell me how this is my fault."

"You should have taken the pin."

"Pin? Oh, that pin. I don't follow you."

"When you didn't take the pin, I knew you didn't believe us. That pin should have had some finger prints on it and you just let everyone handle it."

"Yes, they did, didn't they. The person who sold it to the dropper. And we don't know who else. It probably came from Parisian in the mall. On sale for $39.99. The sales clerk checked and said they have sold about thirteen, and then Dillard's has the same pin and they have sold about ten. No one has records of it. If it came from there. The pin is not exclusive to anyone.

"But perhaps you are right. If you want me to do prints, give it to me and I will have prints run. Prints won't really prove anything. How many people touched it as they were shopping? People do look and don't buy. Give it to me and we'll do prints. But don't get your hopes up."

"Don't get yours up either. I don't have it."

"Where is it?"

"In the dumpster. That's why I was in there. Harvey got this crazy idea he didn't want Mary Ellen to have it and so he threw it away. I was trying to get it back."

"No luck, huh?'

"None."

"Then let's go home."

"You gonna give me a ride?"

Oneal looked at her for a moment. "Yeah," he said reluctantly. "If you smell up my car..."

"Hum! I'm sure you've had worse riding in that car. And I own that car just as much as you do. Besides, you should give me a ride home anyway. If you had done your job to begin with we wouldn't be sitting here now. We might have that dropper in jail." Gladys got up. "Well don't just sit there, let's go. Mary Ellen's at home by herself. It's dark. That nut could show while I'm gone and her there alone."

"The boyfriend is not there?"

Gladys walked in front of his desk, but then she stopped. "Huh!" she mumbled, glancing at Nash, then walked on.

Chapter Eleven

"I can't believe you did that!" Mary Ellen cried. Gladys had just walked through the front door. She pulled her smelly sweater off, started to hang it on the tree, then stopped. She held it in her hand. She wasn't the only thing that had to be washed.

"It's not my fault."

"Not your fault! And just whose fault is it? Just who told you to go climb into a dumpster and get yourself arrested?"

"She didn't get arrested."

"Oh, you stay out of this!" Mary Ellen turned on Nathan. "That's all she needs. A cop for a sidekick who takes her side!"

"I'm not taking anyone's side. I just said she wasn't arrested."

"Thanks to you." She walked toward the living room.

"You leave Officer Oneal out of this. It's Harvey's fault, that's whose fault it is."

Mary Ellen stopped. She didn't turn around. Her hands gripped the edges of her skirt. "Harvey? It's Harvey's fault?" She didn't turn but walked into the living room. Gladys was still in the foyer.

"Well, it is!" cried Gladys.

Nathan Oneal knew it was time he left. He just didn't really know how to leave. He stood in the front hall. Gladys stood near the door that led into the living room. Then Gladys said an unusual thing. "And you still don't know if he's a murderer!"

Nathan decided maybe he should stay just a little longer.

Mary Ellen whirled around. "How dare you accuse him of such! Oh, you have such a petty mind in your old age. If you think for one minute this will keep me from marrying him, you are very wrong!" She stomped out of the room and went upstairs.

Nathan stood staring at Gladys. "You got a reason for saying that? Or is it as she said…you just trying to stop this wedding?"

"I've never said I was trying to stop this wedding. I just think a person should tell it like it is and I say she doesn't know about his dead wife. He's the one who brought up serial killer. What made him think about killers if he isn't one?"

"Mrs. Forsman, what you just said doesn't make a bit of sense. You just brought up murder. Are you a murderer?"

"Don't be ridiculous," she scolded.

"Are you the one sending those roses?"

"Oh—now I see how it is—you're taking the side of Mary Ellen just because you think I'm old and don't have all my senses any more. Well, I'll have you know right now—I'm not sending any roses—or anything else."

"Mrs. Forsman, I know this has to be a difficult time for you—your daughter getting married—left alone."

"You don't know what you're talking about. You

think I'm doing this, don't you? I think it's time you left."
She walked toward the dining room, then stopped. Nathan
started toward the front door. "No wait." Gladys came
back into the hallway. "No sense in us getting miffed.
Come on in and have a seat. Mary Ellen will be down in a
few minutes."

"What?"

"You did come over to help, didn't you?"

"What?"

"I thought so. I'll be right back." She scurried up
stairs. A few minutes later Mary Ellen appeared at the top
of the stairs.

Nathan Oneal looked up. Mary Ellen stood at the
banister looking down. Her hair was a cross between a
blonde and a brunette. What was the term he heard used—
dishwater blonde. That dreadful color the commercial said
no woman wanted. But on Mary Ellen it was kinda pretty.
Her hair touched just above her shoulders, the ends turned
up in a light flip. Bangs touched her forehead. He bet it
was the same cut she had worn since she was twenty. She
was a woman of very few changes. Was that why she was
getting married to a man older than her? He wondered how
many years it was. He looked much older—but then it
might be just hard living.

But Mary Ellen, even with that hairstyle, was pretty.
She had a straight nose, full lips, and soft brown eyes. She
wasn't large. Small boned. Neat waist line. She actually
had a nice figure. He wondered why their paths had never
touched? He had lived in Farley since he was a small child.
Farley is small. Odd. He just never noticed her before.

She moved down the stairs, her dress swaying as she
took the steps.

"Mother said you wanted to talk with me. Something about helping me tonight."

"Well—" He had no real thought about staying, but why not? He didn't have anything he had to do tonight. "Yeah. Thought maybe we could watch for the guy together. Maybe we will get lucky."

"Lucky?"

"Maybe that's not the right word—but if it puts an end to your yellow roses, then maybe it will be a lucky night."

A soft smile touched her lips. "Yes."

They sat on the couch. She on one end; he on the other. Waiting. The TV was off. Gladys was in bed asleep. She never came back down stairs. She took her bath, and went to her room. From there she would watch TV until she fell asleep.

"This is the third night?"

"No, fourth. In some ways it seems as if it has been longer. Seems as if mother and I have argued more these last few days than we have in a lifetime. Some times I worry about her...since daddy died."

"It's hard when a person loses a spouse."

"You?"

"No. My granddad. I watched him. Seemed like he was making it ok until evening rolled around. Suppertime was the hardest. The nights bothered him. I guess that's why he didn't last long after mom-mom was gone. Seven months. I really do believe he grieved himself to death. He said he was eating and when I was there, he would eat a few bites, but then he would get to talking about when mom-mom was there. He just never got past it."

"How long were they married?"

"Sixty-four years."

"Oh, my. No wonder he was lost."

"Yeah. He was eighty-seven—she was ninety. But they were still at home. They were in good health until suddenly it was gone. Almost as if it was like water evaporating from a glass. Couldn't see it going, until it was just gone."

His voice softened, then he grew very quiet. Mary Ellen was quiet. Not wanting to invade his thoughts. Then he spoke. "Your mom...she dearly loves you."

"I know. And I know she means well. But sometimes I just want to grab her and shake her so she will see she doesn't have to live the way she does. That I am leaving. That she must make a new beginning without dad."

"How long has it been?" He was expecting a few years, but it surprised him when Mary Ellen said ten. "Ten! Have you thought about getting her professional help?"

Mary Ellen laughed. It was a slow easy laugh. Nathan smiled.

"What did I say that was funny?"

"Getting mother help. You don't know my mother. No one takes her anywhere that she doesn't want to go. And professional help." She laughed again and shook her head. "I'll let you take her. Then after you have tried, maybe—maybe I might just bandage your wounds." She chuckled.

"In that case, it might be worth the effort."

Mary Ellen blushed. Oh, curse it! Why did she have to blush like some fumbling little teenager? Quickly she moved toward the window.

"What was that? Did you hear that?" She didn't hear anything. She just didn't know what to say to this nice looking man sitting beside her on her sofa in the semi-darkness.

Nathan followed her to the window. He touched her hand as she touched the lace. He shook his head. He moved away from her, leaned against the wall, easing the curtain slightly away from the window so he could see the front porch. He saw nothing. He shook his head again. They waited for a moment. The seconds passed. There was no sound. Silence captured the room. Again he shook his head as he moved the lace slightly.

"There's nothing there," he said softly.

Mary Ellen moved back to the sofa. Nathan stood beside the window. His eyes scanned the yard. It was eleven o'clock. Would the dropper show? If he was, he wished he would come on.

"Bring me a chair from the kitchen. I'm going to sit next to this window. From here I can see from every angle."

Mary Ellen brought a chair from the kitchen. Nathan sat down next to the window his body close to the wall, his finger lifting the curtain lightly. She looked at the top of his head. He had a full head of hair…nice shiny blonde hair.

She shook her head as if to scold herself. She would be glad when she got married and all this was behind her and she stopped noticing men's hair or smile. She wished it was Harvey here and not this officer. She wished Harvey would just tell her let's run away and get married. Then she would have an excuse.

But she didn't really want an excuse. All her life she had dreamed of her wedding day. Her best friend, Melissa Shipon-Meyer was her matron of honor. They had been friends since fourth grade. They became best friends when old Mrs. Shumake had made them stand in the corner for talking. At recess, they deliberately spend the whole recess talking to each other just to get even with Mrs. Shunmake. They discovered they liked each other. They were only talking before because they were arguing over what was the coolest color—blue or purple?

She had a matron of honor, three bridesmaids. Gloria was one of the bridesmaids. Gloria said she would consider it an honor to be a bride's maid in her father's wedding. She had hesitated about asking her, not knowing how she would take it since her mother had only been dead a few months when she and Harvey started dating.

"You really don't have a clue, do you?"

"What?" Nathan brought her out of her thoughts. "Oh. No. I don't."

"That makes it harder. But we will catch him if he keeps this up." She nodded her head. "Why don't you take you a nap on the couch? No sense in both of us losing sleep."

That was nice of him.

"I don't think that would be fair. Besides, the time will pass quicker if we both stay awake. We can talk—help pass the time."

He smiled. "Tell me about your wedding. Is it a large one?"

"Not really. Four attendants. There will be a reception afterward."

"Where are you going on your honeymoon or should I ask. Some times people want that kept a secret."

"No secret. We have thought about several places. Just haven't decided yet. Harvey said it was no big deal.

We should have no problems this time of year."

Nathan nodded his head. He would want to know it was planned if it was his honeymoon. Each to their own.

"Why did your mother say something about murder?"

Because she's a nut, Mary Ellen thought. It made her so mad that her mother made that remark. Instead she said, "Mother just doesn't want me to get married. I even wondered if she was the one sending the flowers but she swore it wasn't her."

Nathan nodded his head. Same question he had asked.

"You don't believe there's any thing to be suspicious about your fiancé's wife's death?"

"No! Of course not. He's a good, honest, decent man. That's just mom blowing off. Don't pay any attention to her. Remember, she was the one you dug out of the dumpster."

He chuckled. "No not me. One of the other officers. She said she couldn't find the pin."

"Would you expect her to. It's probably on the bottom. She's lucky she didn't break her neck in that thing."

"Why did he throw it out?"

"Who? Harvey? He just didn't want me to keep it. He said he would take care of it for me. So he threw it out. Everything would have been fine if mother didn't get this crazy notion she wanted it checked for prints. Do you think it would have really mattered?"

"Never know. Farley knows how to check for prints but you've got to remember this is Farley. Not much to work with. We've got ten officers which is good. But they have to cover the county as well. And it's divided into three shifts. Not a lot of equipment."

"Mayberry."

"Mayberry?"

"That's what mom calls Farley when she's upset about something. Says the law officers are about as sharp as Barney Fife." She laughed. "Not saying much for you, is she?"

"No. Not really. At least she hasn't called me Barney yet."

Mary Ellen laughed again. "But the night is young. You never know when she might come down those stairs and take you by the shirt collar and say, 'Barney, you ain't caught that dropper yet?' Yeah, you best be on your toes."

Nathan grinned as he eased the curtain again. "I wonder if there will be a reason to be on my toes. This fellow keeps either late hours or early hours.

"What time do you go to bed?"

"Different times? Why? You think he comes after we're asleep. That's why we never hear anything?"

"Probably. But then since there isn't a dog, you wouldn't hear anything unless he stumped his toe and yelled."

The clock ticked the hours away. Mary Ellen got another chair and sat beside Nathan as they gazed out the window. Nothing happened. No rose. No one walking down the street. There was nothing stirring on the quiet peaceful street. Around four, Nathan called it a night. If he hurried home, he would get about three or four hours of sleep before reporting for work.

Mary Ellen fell asleep on the couch around five. Her mother woke her at seven.

"Anything?"

Mary Ellen wiped sleep from her eyes as she

answered, "Nothing. Nathan stayed until around four. He had to be at work by eight or so. But there was nothing. Guess he just didn't show last night. Maybe it's over."

She tossed the wrap from her legs. Got up and stretched her back, her arms, and her neck. She moaned. "Man, that old couch slept rough. What do you want for breakfast?"

"Eggs," Gladys replied. She was hungry this morning. Guess it was from all that prowling last night in that dumpster. "And a few slices of bacon too."

Mary Ellen nodded as she moved toward the kitchen. She stopped, turned back and stared hard at the front door. As long as that door wasn't opened, it was ok, yet she had to look. Slowly she moved for the door, opening the heavy oak door. Through the storm door, she saw it lying in the same spot. She eased open the storm door, glancing around, she moved for the rose. The whole time her eyes were scanning the area for any movements. But all was still.

The rose was dry. There was no morning frost on the rose or its wrap. She stared at it, then threw it. It floated across the porch in a downward delicate dive. A small piece of white paper floated down with it.

Chapter Twelve

The phone was ringing. She heard it. She didn't care. She wanted that piece of paper before it was lost. Mary Ellen dashed across the porch and grabbed at the small floating piece of paper. It sailed downward almost as if it were searching for her as she was it. It landed a few steps from her feet. She grabbed it. But then she hesitated. This paper might tell her who the dropper was. Excitement and nerves gnawed at her. Slowly she opened it.

Ten days □

That was all. Ten days? Ten days? What did it mean? What?

Fear grabbed her. Ten days! Ten days was her wedding day.

She looked around. There was no one. Quickly she darted inside.

"Mother!"

Gladys rushed to her daughter. "What is it, baby?" Mary Ellen held out the paper. Gladys took it. "Ten days? Is this all?"

Mary Ellen nodded her head. "Mother, ten days until my wedding."

Gladys grabbed her daughter to her, hugging her. "Now, now. Baby. You just be still. Take a deep breath. It's going to be all right." She led Mary Ellen into the living room. "Here sit down. I'm going to call the police. Didn't you say Officer Oneal was going to work this morning? Fine time for him to go home." Her finger dialed the number. "Officer Oneal." She waited. "Ok. You tell him to call Gladys Forsman just as soon as he comes through those doors. This is important."

She hung up the phone and turned to Mary Ellen. "You ok, baby?"

Mary Ellen looked up at her mother. If she wasn't so worried, it would almost be cute. Her mother was more concerned over her now then she had been in ten years.

Her smile was weak, but still she smiled at her mother. "I'll be ok."

"Sure you will. You're my girl."

Mary Ellen stood. "I need to call Harvey."

That wasn't what she thought she should be doing but Harvey was soon to be her son-in-law. She nodded her head. Mary Ellen went into the kitchen. She couldn't hear her words. Her voice was too low.

"Harvey, there was a note with the rose this morning. It said, ten days. That's what was written on a small piece of paper. Ten Days."

"What do you think it means?"

"Ten days is our wedding day." Harvey didn't say anything. "Harvey?"

"I heard you. Have you called the police?"

"Yes. Mother called for Nathan."

Silence.

"Harvey?"

"Yes."

"Did you hear me?"

"I heard you. I'll be there in a few minutes."

Harvey arrived within fifteen minutes. That was the fastest he had ever made it, Gladys decided. She decided it was because of Nathan. That one little word threw a new image before his eyes, and he got himself over here pronto. Well, that's good. He should have been here last night. Gloria could have chosen another night to go out.

He came in, stood in the hallway with his hat, speaking to Mary Ellen in a low tone. Then he moved into the living room and sat down in the comfortable chair.

"Harvey would you like some coffee. I haven't cooked anything to eat yet. But there is some coffee made."

"No, thank you. Just bring me that note. I want to see it."

"I don't know about that." Gladys came out of the kitchen with a mug of coffee.

"And what do you mean by that, Mrs. Forsman? I do believe as Mary Ellen's husband to be, it is my duty to look out for her."

And where were you last night? You weren't too concern last night.

"I don't think we should handle it. They may want to check for prints."

"But, mother, we handled it."

"And all the more reason why it shouldn't be handled any more then necessary."

Harvey's eyes bored into Gladys. He did not like this

woman. He was civil to her because of Mary Ellen. How could a gentle creature as Mary Ellen come from this despicable being, Gladys Forsman?

Gladys smiled at Harvey. Sipped her coffee, her eyes never leaving his. Harvey returned her smile.

"Mother, what did you do with the paper?"

"It's on the piano." Then a thought went through her mind. Let him handle it. She would have his prints. Maybe she could get Nathan to run his prints. That's what *Kinsey* would do. Get her confidant in the police department to help her out.

Mary Ellen found the note and gave it to Harvey. He looked at it as if it were a long lengthy note instead of two words.

"Off a computer."

"Yes."

Real whiz here, Gladys declared. Wonder how the top-notch reporter figured that one?

"I believe you should see the DA."

"Why?"

"You need to put a little pressure on that cop. He's not doing enough."

"He's doing all he can. He stayed here until four this morning," Gladys informed.

Mary Ellen looked at her mother as a parent does a misbehaving child. Gladys didn't read the message.

"He seemed determined to help. The dropper just came after he left. The poor man had to be at work by eight—wasn't that what you said Mary Ellen? Anyway, looks like it would have been better if he had just stayed."

"Nathan should be here right away," Mary Ellen said.

Harvey didn't say anything. He cut cold eyes up at

Mary Ellen.

She didn't like it when he looked at her like that. She wanted to sit on the ottoman and everything be ok. He could stroke her hair, telling her what time he would come by in the evening. That's how it was five days ago. Just the two of them, sitting in the living room.

But within five days her world had turned upside down. Her mother was impossible. Some horrible person was tormenting her mind, and her wedding bliss was being threatened. She was beginning to feel like Harvey didn't trust her any more. He kept giving her these looks or else silence.

"This Nathan fellow—is that your officer?"

"Oh yes. Nathan Oneal. One of Farley' finest," Gladys answered.

This woman watched too much TV.

"When did he say he would be here?"

"Well, I didn't get a chance to speak to him," Gladys replied.

"And what about you, Mary Ellen."

"Oh, she didn't speak to…"

"I was speaking to Mary Ellen." He turned to Mary Ellen. "What about it? Mary Ellen. Did your officer say anything last night."

Her officer? He wasn't her officer. She never saw a side like this before with Harvey. He was always so quiet, gentle.

The doorbell buzzed.

"Oh, there he is." Gladys scrambled for the door faster than she had ever moved. It was eight o'clock by the clock in the front hall. Nathan came over as soon as he got her call. That boy was doing all right. She opened the door. It wasn't Nathan.

"I have a package for Mary Ellen Forsman." It was the deliveryman again. With another box.

"That does it!" Harvey shouted from the living room. Abruptly he was at the front door. He pushed her aside, grabbed the package, tossing it out the door. He glared at the deliveryman. "Don't bring anything else here. Do I make myself clear?"

"Hey—hold on there!" Nathan shouted as he dodged the box as he walked up the sidewalk. "Take it ease there! This isn't the way. We need that. Where's Mary Ellen?"

"You don't need Mary Ellen! You need to speak with me. I am Mary Ellen's spokesman from now on."

"Now, wait a minute, Harvey. You can't do that. You want to throw everything away. How are we going to catch the dropper if you keep throwing everything away? You threw out the pin. I never did find it."

"What are you talking about?"

"I searched that dumpster. I couldn't find it," Gladys replied curtly.

"Well—well that's your fault. Not mine."

Gladys propped her hands on her hips. "Now wait a minute here. Just one darn minute. I have you know, it's your fault for throwing it out—just like you did that box lying in the front yard."

She grabbed the pen from the startled man standing on the front porch. "Give me that pad." She signed the clipboard form. "Now, that's mine."

She marched down the front steps and took the package from Nathan who had picked it up out of the yard. She spotted David Petrie coming out of his mother's house. He threw up his hand at Gladys, but she didn't respond.

"This package is now mine. I signed for it. And..." she turned to Harvey, "...you won't throw this one away,"

"Gladys, let me see the box." Nathan held out his hand. Gladys looked at Harvey. He turned his head away. She handed the box to Nathan.

Inside the box was a wooden box with roses cut into the lid. Nathan removed the lid. The red velvet lined box contained *Brighton's Callie* two-toned heart earrings and a watch. And a *Callie* two-tone heart necklace.

Nathan looked up at Mary Ellen. "Any thoughts to whom?"

She didn't touch the box or the items. Slowly she shook her head and looked at Gladys. "Mother, who would be doing this?"

"No idea."

Harvey stared at the contents. "Hearts. Always hearts."

"What do you mean, Harvey?" Nathan asked.

"Candy, flowers, the vase was heart shaped at the top, and now more hearts." He took a deep breath before he turned to Mary Ellen. His words slow, tense. "Mary Ellen. I want to know...is there someone else...have you got someone else on the side?"

"How could you ask me that?" she gasped. "No. No." She ran into the living room, fell down into the big comfortable chair and covered her face with her hands as the tears flowed.

"Then why is someone spending all this money on you?" he demanded as he followed her into the room.

More than you ever spent, thought Gladys, but she decided to let the remark slide. The hot fire needed no more fuel.

"I won't put up with a wife that hides things. I went through that with Mildred. Never knowing what she was up to. I won't do it again." He stood over her now, his hat still in his hand. Mary Ellen did not look up, but kept her face buried in her hands.

He suddenly threw his hat across the room, grabbed her with his hands and pulled her up out of the chair. "Look at me!" he shouted, "Look at me and tell me who it is!"

Gladys was behind him before he knew she was in the room. Her hand slapped hard across his face, leaving a red mark and a stinging face. He dropped Mary Ellen back into the chair, and turned on Gladys.

"What in the devil do you think you're doing?" he shouted, his left hand touching his face. Nathan still stood by the front door waiting to see what the next move would be. If Gladys was going to put Harvey in his place, he wouldn't stop her, but Harvey must not touch Gladys. He waited.

"You will not touch my daughter that way!" she barked.

"You won't tell me what I can do. In ten days your daughter will be my wife…she won't be your baby to dictate any longer."

"She will always be my baby!'

"Not when we're…"

"Stop it! Stop it!" Mary Ellen jumped up, shoving aside Harvey and her mother. "Just leave me alone. That's all I want!" she shouted. She dashed from the room and out the door.

"Why didn't you stop her," Gladys demanded of Nathan, but he just shrugged.

"I think she needed out of here," he said.

Mary Ellen ran down the steps, across the grass onto the sidewalk. She ran, tears falling, blinding her, but she ran. She wanted away from all of them. Away from all the questions. Away from the gifts. She wanted to escape it all.

She didn't see the little red sport car pull up along side her.

"Hey."

She kept running.

"Hey."

She didn't slow nor look.

"Mary Ellen." It was David. Her pace slowed. "El. El. It's me. Stop."

She stopped. She lifted her wet face upward.

David pulled the car over, then got out. "What's wrong, babe?" He caught her elbows, pulling her close to him, enveloping her with his arms. She laid her wet face on his chest crying into his shoulder. He placed his hand on the back of her head, stroking her hair. "Go ahead and cry baby. Cry it all out."

She cried—and cried. Finally, she lifted a red face and moist eyes to meet his. He smiled softly at her. Then he took one finger and wiped under her eyes.

"Feel any better."

She swallowed. A weak smile touched her lips. "A little."

"Good. Come on." He opened the car door. She slid into the passenger seat. After he closed the door, he went around the car and got in beside her.

"Where are we going?"

"Does it matter?"

No, it didn't. She just wanted away. Away from her mother, from Harvey, the evil person who was doing all this to her. Anywhere. But she didn't answer as he pulled the car away from the curb.

Chapter Thirteen

"Now," he said as they headed across town. In ten minutes they were out of town, and he finished the sentence. "I have decided what you need to do is go with me to Africa." She laughed. "I'm serious. That's where I will be going next week. And as my co-pilot, I think you should come with me. We can finish those adventures we began twenty-five years ago."

She laughed again. "Oh, I see how it's going to be, I'm going to be the co-pilot again, huh."

He laughed. "Sure. All pilots need a good co-pilot."

"And what happens when we land?"

"Oh, we'll see." He smiled. Those pearly white teeth gleaming in the sunlight. He sped the car onto the open highway.

"I heard them...yelling. What's going on El? You're getting married in a few days. This is supposed to be the happiest time of your life."

"And it was."

"What do you mean—was?"

"Someone, I don't know who, has decided to send me flowers—a single yellow rose for the last four days—and gifts. I don't know why. I don't know who."

"A yellow rose?" He kept his eyes on the road. "A yellow rose means joy—peace. That's odd."

"There's no joy or peace in those roses. It is some nut!"

"Maybe an old boyfriend who doesn't want you to get married. Maybe he is trying to tell you that you're marrying the wrong guy."

"What old boyfriends?" She cut her eyes to him. "You were the only old boyfriend and you left me when you were twelve." She smiled. "Have you been carrying a torch for me all these years, David? Is that what it is?"

He laughed. "Never out of my heart."

Together they laughed. It was a warm happy laugh. One she enjoyed. She had not thought about it in a long time, but she missed David when he moved off to college, moved away and got married. As long as they were in school, at first she kept thinking he would come back over. Then after awhile, he stopped speaking even when he saw her in the school hallways. He just tossed up his hand and kept walking. So many years ago. What would life have been like if he had been hers?

She shook her head slightly. Harvey. What was she saying? She loved Harvey. She was marrying Harvey.

He glanced at her. "You ok?"

"Yeah, sure."

He drove until they went up on the Hill. From here they could look down on Farley. They were only about a mile from town. There was a small stream that ran through the hill, a waterfall on a drop off as the stream flowed away from town. A hillside with tree and a waterfall. No wonder it was a favorite spot for lovers. Perfect for summer picnics…blankets on the ground picnics with wild flowers all around.

"Remember when we used to play up here?"

Yeah, she remembered. They made their camp by the stream and played cowboys. This was their outlaw hideout from the posses. They also had two space ships. One in her backyard and one up on the Hill in a large sweet gum tree.

The branches were close enough to the ground to climb up into the big tree, and limbs that went high into the sky. Their space ship had two levels; the lower level had wide boards for the floor, which they had nailed into the tree limbs. But the second level, the command control, had only one board that rested between two limbs. This was the seat the pilot sat on, the controls in his hands. The control panel was an aluminum pie pan nailed to a stick.

He was always the pilot, but he would allow her to take the controls while he checked out the danger below. Sometimes there were fires in the level below that he had to put out or fight off space aliens that were trying to get onto their ship as she flew them through space.

Once the danger passed, he returned for the controls and she always sat beside him as his co-pilot.

"Pretty up here, isn't it."

"Um."

"Remember the Galley 4000?"

She smiled. "How could I forget. The fastest, most powerful, sleekest space ship in the universe."

"Silver—trimmed in metallic blue."

She laughed. "I wanted pink."

"Yeah." He chuckled. "Good thing I was the commander or we would have been the Pink Spacey."

"Well, I will have to admit Blue Eagles did sound

better."

"Yes, and as your commander, I order you to tell me what's bothering you." She hesitated. "I could hear all the yelling even from my yard. What gives? Who do you think is behind the roses and gifts?"

"I haven't a clue. I just know he has made my life miserable these last few days."

His finger touched her hand; lightly it flowed upward on her arm. "El, it's important that you sort through all the people who come into your life. When you do, there will be this one person who stands out and you will know who it is sending the flowers."

She looked into his warm eyes. He had been such a dear friend so many years ago.

"No one stands out. I go to church, give lessons, and go to the market. Harvey and I stay in most evenings. We don't really go out that much. There is no reason why someone would be doing this."

"There is always a reason. You just haven't thought it through. You contemplate on the why too much and not enough on whom you really know. Think. Who did you see the first day you found the rose?"

"No one. I got up. There is a rose on the front porch. I thought Harvey sent it. He was over the night before. But when I told him about it, he didn't know what I was talking about. Then the candy came.

"Mother ate the candy. Can you believe that? Said why throw away good candy."

"Maybe it's your mother. Maybe she doesn't want you to get married and if this causes problems between you and Harvey, the wedding would be called off."

"I thought that too. But when I questioned her, she

swore it wasn't her."

"Would she tell you if it were?"

Mary Ellen sat silent for a moment, her eyes wandering over the Hill. Without looking at David, she answered, "I don't think mother would lie to me about it. I know she isn't the woman you knew when we were kids. She changed after daddy died. It's almost as if she just stopped living and pulled her world in around her. Closed it all up, and just put it away. Now, she just drifts through each day with her soaps."

She turned to David. "You know, I guess I have seen more spirit out of her in these last few days than I have in the last ten years. Odd, isn't it?"

David shrugged his shoulders. His finger strolled back down her arm. Mary Ellen pushed the feeling from her mind that were stirring within her.

He leaned over close to her. "El, what about you?"

"What about me?"

"What do you want?" He whispered the words into her hair, he breathed slowly, softly.

His breath warmed her ear, her cheek. A feeling rushed across her before she could stop it. It was excitement. That was bad. What made it worse—she didn't blush.

His lips touched hers. Soft, gentle. Demanding nothing from her. Again, and again. Soft. Light. Gentle kisses on her lips. She felt her hand reach up to his cheek, touching his face lightly, her lips returning his kisses.

Then she jerked away.

"What's wrong, El."

"I'm engaged to be married. That's what's wrong."

"But El,"

"No, David, no. I won't let you do this to me."

"What are you talking about? Do what?"

"You haven't changed. It's always been about what you wanted."

"Ah, come on, El, we were kids."

"Do you remember the space ship control panel?"

"Sure."

"You never trusted me to fly the space ship. You were the one in control. Even when you didn't want to play in the space ship, you wouldn't let me."

"How could I have stopped you? It was a tree."

"You took the control panel home with you every day. You never left it in the space ship. You said if I flew the ship alone, I would get lost."

He laughed. "El, that was a long time ago." He pulled her up close to him to kiss her again, but she turned her face away. "El, come on. I just want to hold you."

"No. I'm engaged. I shouldn't have kissed you. I'm sorry."

"And I should have never let you go years ago."

"But you did. Just like you took the control panel."

"Ah, come on, El. We were ten. It was just a stick. All you had to do was just get another stick and put an aluminum pie pan on for the wheel. It wasn't real, El."

He caught her hand in his. Electricity flashed through her. Quickly she pulled her hand away.

"And neither is this. We need to go."

"No. Let's talk. We can't leave it like this."

He was still the boss. But she wasn't ten now. She opened the car door.

"Fine. I can walk back."

"El, no."

She began to walk back down the road. He started the

car and followed her.

"El, get in the car."

"No. You bossed me when we were kids. You took the control panel and broke my young heart."

"El, it was just a stick—just a stick! Why didn't you just get another stick?" The car followed closely.

She whirled. "You still don't understand. It wasn't just a stick. It was the control panel of our space ship. It was ours, not just yours! Now here you come after a lifetime of not seeing you and we're best buddies again! In ten days I'm getting married. In less then a week, you're leaving for Africa, and this time I'm in control of what I do—not you. I won't cheat on Harvey just so you can have your fun."

"I'm sorry. I won't touch you, just get in the car. You can't walk back into town. Everyone who sees you will wonder where you've been. Walking down the road like this. Come on."

She knew he was telling the truth. Farley watched all of Farley. She stopped. He stopped the car. She stood there for a moment, just looking at him, angry at herself for letting him stir emotions within her. Angry with him for kissing her in the first place. He knew she was engaged. He made her forget that fact for a moment.

She opened the car door, and slumped into the seat. "Alright. Let's go." He smiled. "And get rid of that smile. I'm still angry at you."

"Over the space panel?" Again he smiled mischievously.

She wanted to laugh. But she refused. It would just remind her of how handsome and charming he was. And how forbidden.

Chapter Fourteen

Mary Ellen walked across David's front yard and into her own. She wanted to hurry, yet she couldn't. Her heart was heavy. Her spirit tired. David offered to drop her off right at her door, but she refused. There was no point in that. As she entered her yard, her steps slowed even more. She walked up the wide doorsteps. The house was quiet. Harvey's car wasn't in the drive. She crossed the long wide porch and eased open the front door.

Slowly she closed the door.

"Is that you, Mary Ellen?" Gladys called from the living room. Mary Ellen could see her from the foyer. As always, she was in the chair, TV on.

"Yes, mother, it's me." She started for the stairs, but Gladys came into the hallway.

"I'm sorry."

"And just where did you go?"

"David. We went for a ride."

"Really? Seems like David just keeps popping up."

"I'm tired, mother. I'm going upstairs to lie down for awhile. If anything happens, anyone calls, whatever—I'm not here."

"Harvey said for you to call him."

"I will later."

"He said just as soon as you got into the house."

"Later." She placed her hand upon the banister, her back to Gladys.

"He sure didn't like you running out. Said to tell you to call him immediately. Immediately."

With her hand on the banister, Mary Ellen pulled herself up the stairs.

"What do you want me to tell him if he calls?"

Mary Ellen didn't answer. Wearily she climbed the stairs.

"Ok," Gladys called. Well guess that left the barn door wide open to tell Mr. Broyhill just any old thing she wanted to. Not that she would lie. But then she wouldn't have too.

Out with David, huh?

Chapter Fifteen

"Daddy, I don't understand what you're so upset about," Gloria spoke into the phone. She had the twins ready for Mother's Day out at the church and was in a hurry to get out the door. Besides, she wasn't really interested in why Mary Ellen was crying. Mary Ellen was her father's responsibility.

"I don't know where she went. She was all upset. It's that mother of hers. That woman has got to go. Once this wedding is over, she's gone."

"Daddy, Mary Ellen comes with that mother. You might as well accept that." He should have thought about that before he got involved with her. Mom gone only a few months and he's gets involved with a woman young enough to be his daughter!

"No. I don't accept anything I don't like, and I don't like that woman."

Gloria sighed. "Dad, I've got to go. Mary Ellen will be back. All tears dried. So she needed to get out of the house? Don't worry." She brushed it off.

"You don't get it, do you? Someone keeps sending her flowers and gifts. I don't know if she is in danger or if it's just an old boyfriend."

"Ha! What I've heard about Mary Ellen Forsman there has never been another boyfriend. There was no one before you, you have no competition. So stop worrying."

"It's probably that mother."

"Perhaps." She fastened the twin's jackets. "Listen, dad, I've got to run." Before he could say another word she hung up the phone.

Harvey replaced the receiver. There were papers covering his desk—papers he needed to type up for the obituary page, but he couldn't get Mary Ellen out of his thoughts. She was always such a meek little creature— hanging onto his every word, every movement. He knew without her telling she had never been with a man. He wanted to hear her say it though, so he hinted. Telling her, he could tell she was a lady—not a worldly woman. She was as delicate as the morning dew that touched the roses.

He snapped the pencil in his hands. Roses. Maybe there had been more than just morning dew touching those roses!

He dialed Mary Ellen's number. Gladys answered.

"Is she back?"

"Yes."

"Tell her I want to speak to her."

"She said she wasn't taking any calls."

"She'll take mine."

"That's not what she said. She said didn't matter who called, or what happened. Do not bother her with it. That's what she said."

"Go tell her I want to speak to her."

"I can't go against what she asked."

He snapped another pencil between his fingers. Why not? You always go against what she says.

"Tell her I called."

"I will. She will probably be up soon. She has lessons later this afternoon. Church tonight. I don't know if she and David have any plans after lunch or not."

"What?"

Gladys smiled. She could hear the edge in his voice, the strain to keep it steady.

"I said, I don't know if she and David have any other plans for the day or not."

"David?"

"Yeah, he's next door." She waited just for a moment then continued. "David is Mrs. Petrie's son. Mary Ellen grew up with him."

"What was he doing over there this morning?"

"Oh, he wasn't. When Mary Ellen got upset, she and David ended up together. They went for a ride. But I don't think she has any other plans with him today. But I'll ask when she gets up if you like."

What was Mary Ellen doing with this Petrie guy again? Didn't I tell her to stay away from him the other day?

"Harvey?"

He wasn't about to ask this old bat anything about this. But Mary Ellen would be hearing about it!

"Just tell her I called." He hung up.

Gladys replaced the phone receiver to the wall. Well, wasn't that a nice call. She smiled as she went into the foyer, removed her sweater and purse. She went to the garage, and backed the Ford out of the garage.

She eased down the drive. It's been a long time since she'd driven this car. In her young days she owned a black '51 Chevy Fleetline, fender skirt—blinder and plenty of chrome. She hated that car.

She bought it her first year out of high school after she got a job at Wally's Five & Dime on Main Street. Her dad told her he had the perfect car for her. The year was August. 1961, and she had been working since June— saving every penny she could get for her dream car, Ford Thunderbird. The perfect car would be a new Thunderbird, but she would settle. A '55 or '57 would work. They were hot!

She would never forget that day. Her daddy came into the house from work, pitched his hat onto the kitchen table and told her he knew just the car for her. He worked at Lee's Clothing store on the square, and he saw everyone in Farley. And he knew she was saving for a car.

When she told him she wanted a Thunderbird, he just smiled. She had mistakenly taken that smile to mean he was in agreement. He didn't think like her, though. She was eighteen, she wanted a sporty little car that she could whirl around in. She would be center stage as her hair blew in the wind as she cruised around Farley's town square.

Then he broke the news to her. That was how she always viewed it. Broke the news to her.

Her Aunt Agnes had been in the store that day, asking him if he knew of anyone who might be interested in buying a car. Herbert was buying them a new Oldsmobile and they were selling their old car.

And that's what it looked like. An old car left over from some long lost century before they ever started building cars in this country. It resembled a black hunched-over bug. Like a big black boll weevil crawling down the road. She didn't want it. But her daddy told her what a good car it was…that he had already told her aunt that she would be right over to look at it. There was no way around it. And when they got there, Aunt Agnes went on and on about what a good deal they were giving her.

But she didn't want it.

She bought it, though. Drove it for two years, two years! Two long years to prove just how much she appreciated that car. It took all her money for gas, for little tune-ups that her dad kept telling her meant nothing. That all cars had bugs that you had to work out. He just never could admit he had helped her buy a bomb!

Then she began dating Norbert and boom. They got married. And she had to drive that old clunker another two years because they couldn't afford another one for her. She worked, but her money didn't go for cars any longer. She couldn't save every penny any more. Married life was different. Just before Mary Ellen was born, the car finally died.

It died and she laughed. She was so thankful. But the one thing she forgot. If they didn't have the money to buy another car while she was working, what made her think just because her car died she would get another one? She gave birth to Mary Ellen, and never worked again, nor did she ever own her own car again. Norbert was always buying new cars, and the car was just as much hers as his, but she never had her car. Until now.

With Norbert gone, his '93 Ford Thunderbird, was now hers. She just didn't drive any longer. Mary Ellen did.

She wondered why Mary Ellen never mentioned buying a car? Even when she went off to college, she never mentioned wanting a car. Norbert never mentioned it either. Mary Ellen was a good girl…a little too quiet sometimes…but a good girl. Maybe she should have told her daddy she wanted her own car. She was twenty-four when he died. She should have told him she wanted her own car. Yeah, she should have told him, Gladys decided as she drove down Carridale Street toward the police department.

Nathan Oneal didn't see Gladys when she came through the glass door at the station. But Gladys saw him. She marched to his desk, dropped her purse on top of his desk, then planted herself in the chair directly across from him.

"Mrs. Forsman, I didn't know you were coming in."

"Neither did I. What did you find out?"

"Nothing. Bought over the counter at one of the local stores in the mall. No record. There never is. This person is very cagey."

"Have you any idea why?"

"I hate to tell you this, but no. Farley is a peaceful little town. There has never been a report of anyone stalking someone. I really don't know what to make of it. Your daughter lives a very quiet life."

Gladys smiled. "Pretty little thing, isn't she?"

Nathan tilted his head slightly, his eyes glancing at his desk. He wasn't expecting that. Yeah, she was pretty. He wondered why she had not married in the past. Surely there had been offers. He figured she was one of those women who were very picky. But then he questioned why Harvey. He just didn't see what she saw in him.

He looked up. A slight smile touched his mouth. "You didn't come here to talk to me about how pretty your daughter is, did you?"

Gladys smiled back at the pretty mouth. "No, I didn't." She glanced around as if she was looking for someone. Then she leaned in just a little. "I want you to do something for me."

"What?" Coming from this woman there was no telling.

"I want you to run Harvey's prints off that note. He handled it. Run his prints for me."

"Why?"

"Causes he's marrying my daughter in ten days and I want to make sure he doesn't have a police record. A serial killer or something. You do know his wife died?"

"How?"

"He says cancer. But it was shortly after they moved here that she became sick. You do know you can give a person just enough arsenic and they will die a painful death and it's hard to detect?"

"And you think he gave her arsenic?"

"I'm saying I want to know more about this man."

"Why?"

"What do you mean, why? I told you why?"

"No, you told me your daughter was getting married in ten days, but you didn't tell me why you decided now to wonder about the man she is marrying. What changed your mind?

"The gifts made me begin to wonder." She leaned back in her chair. "If I'm honest, I never really thought it would go this far. He takes her home from church a few times. His wife had not been dead that long. I actually thought Mary Ellen would grow weary of him. He is such a bore.

"But she didn't. It was like she was smitten by him and the more he came around the more she invited him. And then there she was. A ring on her finger. A wedding was being planned. She spent two thousand dollars for the dress. I couldn't believe it. Still don't."

"But that's not grounds to think he killed his wife."

"Listen to me. This man moves to this small two bit Mayberry of a town. Just him and his wife. They leave Denver—or so he says—where he was working on a larger newspaper. He takes a job at the one and only Farley paper. Then wham! His wife is dead. He has left his home; his family to come here?"

When she put it like that, it even made him wonder. But no one has even hinted that Harvey Broyhill had a mysterious past. Or anything about his wife's death.

"Mrs. Forsman…"

"Oh, please, call me Gladys. After all we've been through." Gladys tossed her hand toward him.

"Ok. Gladys. I want you to think about something for me. Are you suspicious of this person, who is marrying your daughter, because you don't like him or because you really do believe he is capable of murder?"

"Oh, I get it—you think I'm just this crazy old woman who has nothing better to do with her time then to waste yours. Well you hear me and you hear me good, Mr. Law Officer, I know what I'm saying and why I'm saying it. Just because no one else is intelligent enough to see it, don't mean I have to be blind too.

"I'm telling you that man needs to be checked out. If you don't want to, I'll do it myself." She grabbed her purse from Nathan's desk, jumped up from her chair.

"Now wait a minute, Gladys. No sense in getting all upset. I just want you to look at it with a clear conscience. Don't jump him, just because he might not be your favorite son-in-law."

He took a pen and a clean sheet of paper. "Just sit back down," he said and gestured toward the chair. "First of all, do you know which paper he worked with in Denver?"

"No. He said it was a small paper in Denver."

"Ok. This is what I will do. I will check out a few things in Denver. But in the meantime I want you to just keep quiet on everything. Stop giving him a hard time. Stop upsetting Mary Ellen. Keep any and all flowers or gifts Mary Ellen gets from her secret visitor." He looked up from his writing. "And you don't let Harvey throw anything away. Nothing. You understand?"

A smile that was pure delight touched her lips. "Oh, I understand alright...and believe me...so will he."

Chapter Sixteen

She was angry with David. He should not have kissed her. She should have never kissed him. She was angry with him for the emotions he stirred within her. No one but Harvey had stirred emotions in her...but then no one had ever kissed her except Harvey. And now David.

What was he trying to prove? That he was still the heartthrob of Farley? She didn't need this, she had enough to contend with. In ten days she would be married.

Her fingers touched the piano keys as the music filled the church sanctuary. She always played as the parishioners arrived for the Wednesday night prayer service. There were usually only about twenty, maybe twenty-five or so people who would be there for a Wednesday night service. The membership of Farley Baptist Church was only 137, but that was pretty good since there wasn't but about 1500 people in Farley—give or take.

The music flowed and it seemed so peaceful, but her heart wasn't. She actually wished she was somewhere else. Three people had already asked her about the wedding, wanting to know how everything was coming along. She just said fine. No mention of the nut leaving her packages and yellow roses, making her life miserable. In ten days she was getting married—supposed to be the happiest time of her life.

Softly she continued to play, hoping the music would drift her mind to a peaceful place. She didn't see Gloria move in behind her until she leaned over, whispering something in her ear. She saw it, but she couldn't believe it. She might have not even seen it if it had not brushed against her cheek as Gloria leaned forward. She heard Gloria's words but she could not concentrate on what she was saying. All she could focus on was Gloria's chest.

Red rubies were pinned to her sweater on the left side. Bright red rubies in a heart-shaped pin just over her heart!

She was saying something—what was she saying?

"When you're finished playing, would you mind staying in the nursery? Alice Louise was scheduled to, but she's not coming."

Mary Ellen nodded her head. That pin! Harvey said he threw it away. That can't be the same pin. Could it? There are pins like that in the mall. That wasn't the only one. He wouldn't have given it to her. He wouldn't do that.

Oh, if her mother sees that pin! She'll ask. If she wasn't such a coward, she would ask herself. But she couldn't do that. If it turned out that she bought it or Ben gave it to her, she would feel like a fool. And Harvey would get mad!

How odd though. The very pin that she got—that Harvey said he threw away—one just like it is pinned to Gloria's sweater.

She glanced up. Gloria was gone. Maybe she would be in the back. She would hate for her mother to ask about it. Her mother wouldn't care who heard her ask either. Best just not say anything.

The music didn't soothe her soul as it usually did. These last few days nothing soothed her.

She glanced at her watch. It was seven. This would be her last song. The preacher would be stepping forward. The service would begin. He would ask for prayer request. Oh, did she had requests! But they were private.

Pray that whoever the nut was leaving her roses would stop. Pray that Harvey would not ever find out about David's kiss.

Darn. She shouldn't have thought about that. She could feel herself blushing. Oh, what kind of woman was she becoming?

She finished the song, and moving from the piano, she sat next to Harvey, who was sitting on the third pew. Her mother was somewhere toward the back. She never sat up front.

She would be glad when this evening was over. She wanted to go home. She didn't even want Harvey to take her home. The evening was nice, not too cool. A perfect night for lovers to sit outside and gaze up at the stars, but still, she didn't want him coming to the house tonight.

She leaned over and whispered. "I have such a headache."

He patted her right arm. "Poor dear. Do we need to leave?"

She shook her head. Not the remark she wanted to hear. She was getting pretty good at lying, though. Not a characteristic that she actually wanted. She had never told so many lies, felt so many indecent emotions in her life. And just ten days before her marriage.

She never thought it would be like this. All the excitement had been stolen from her. She was weary of this person who sent her the gifts she once would have coveted.

She pulled at the edge of her Bible. The edges were frayed from years of use. Not that she was constantly reading her Bible though. She knew she should. Suddenly she felt so guilty. And she didn't know why.

Harvey placed his hand on hers. She looked up into his eyes. He smiled softly, shaking his head slightly. She let her fingers rest. Then she remembered, she had to stay in the nursery. She whispered the words to him and quickly made her departure.

At eight o'clock they were standing on her front porch. Her mother had insisted on walking home. They offered her a ride, but she wouldn't hear of it. Mary Ellen held her small handbag in her left hand, her right hand resting on the porch column next to the wide sandstone doorsteps. She knew she should ask him in, but tonight she just didn't want to. If she did, she would end up asking him about the pin. And she didn't want to argue about it. If he did, she wanted to know why; if not, she wanted to know that too. But it would not be that clean cut. It would be an argument. His anger of her doubting him would over shadow everything.

"Harvey, please forgive me for not having you in for a glass of tea or something. But my head isn't any better. The best thing I could do is just get a good night's rest."

"Yes, I guess that would be best." He held his hat so it dangled between his fingers. "I don't want you sick. I guess that also means you aren't planning on waiting on your mystery person tonight?"

She had not even thought about that. She didn't want to sit up tonight. It did no good last night, and she was tired. She didn't want to let it slip about the pin. She just wanted him to go home, asking her no more questions.

"No, I don't believe so. It served little purpose."

"I saw none," he rebuked. "That officer—he's not coming over tonight, is he?"

"Nathan?   No, I haven't talked to him since this morning."

Harvey leaned over and gave her a quick peck on the forehead. This time last week she would have insisted he come into the house. This time last week she would have been hoping for a warm kiss on her lips. Tonight she didn't even want the peck on her forehead.

She smiled. "Good night, Harvey."

He returned her smile. "You sleep well. I'll call in the morning to check on you." She nodded her head, then went into the house.

Harvey turned and went down the sandstone steps. His eyes glanced next door. In the semi-darkness he could not tell if the red sport car was there or not. When he reached his car, he gave one last glance. From the street light, he could make out most of the yard. He didn't see any sport car. As he backed out of the drive, he wondered if it was in the garage.

It surprised him that Mary Ellen didn't ask him in. She said she had a headache, but usually she was so eager for him to come in that a headache shouldn't have stopped her. Mary Ellen was such an innocent woman. She wouldn't lie about something like a headache. It would never enter her mind to lie.

Mildred would have though. He learned early on in their marriage Mildred lied to him. He never caught her in but one lie. But if there was one, there were others. That only stood to reason. Once a liar—always a liar.

The car moved slowly down the street, but he wasn't conscious of where he was going. It was as if the car was on autopilot as the driver drifted back into another time when he was in the eleventh grade, and he met Mildred in algebra class. On that first day he discovered she and his best friend Kinkade were neighbors, had been all their lives. She lived two houses down from Kinkade, but he had never met her. He and Kinkade had been best friends since the sixth grade. For five years he had been in and out of Kinkade's house and never noticed the girl next door. But he noticed her now, and he wanted to know this girl—really know her.

She was so pretty with that long black hair, a nice figure, and there was no girl he wanted to score with as he did with her. He had hoped in the beginning that she was an easy mark. Was he ever wrong! She let him know right quick if that was what he was after, he could just look elsewhere.

A pretty girl with good morals that believed in waiting until they were married. They were married in eight months after they graduated high school, but on their wedding night, he wondered about her. He wasn't sure why, but he wondered. He had always heard a virgin bled, but he didn't know if that was true or not. He'd never had a virgin before. All the girls he had been with were known as easy marks, and there hadn't been that many. He wanted a virgin for his wife—thought she was. Until that night.

Mildred told him that not all virgins bleed a lot. That was why there was no blood. She swore it was her first time, then she cried. The very idea he would even suggest such! She acted like he thought a virgin would be, shy, not sure of herself, a little scared.

Then he found it. They had been married five years when Mildred had gone to the grocery store with the babies. He was working seconds at the mill and got up around twelve. The house was empty. He knew where Mildred was, it was Thursday. She always bought groceries on Thursday afternoon. He went into the kitchen to fix himself a sandwich and there it was. Plain as day. He saw it through the white garbage bag. Her dairy! The one she never let him read. The one she kept all through high school. She was throwing it away.

He opened the bag, pulled it out. Why didn't she take out the garbage before she left? Did she leave it on purpose?

He opened the small red cloth dairy. The first entrance was when she was in eighth grade, and she had a crush on a boy by the name of Billy. It was just silly rambling about the school, girl talk, and exams. Her dreams, her hopes were spilled out onto the pages. Kinda boring really.

Until he got to April 22nd. She was in the eleventh grade. She had written it in a sign language. He would never forget those words. 'One passed through life without others noticing the changes. But I know. No one else will ever know, but I will always know. *Today the rose petals fell'*.

He read it twice. He didn't fully understand at first. But then there was that nagging suspicion from their wedding night.

His anger erupted into a murderous rage as he threw the book across the room. It sailed like a speeding bullet into the air and slammed into the refrigerator, bounced off and landed back at his feet. He grabbed it up, cursing, he threw the book into the kitchen sink, grabbed the cooking oil, doused it on top and set it aflame. The lying whore!

When Mildred walked through the back door thirty minutes later, she found her kitchen sink covered in black soot.

She sat the bag of groceries down on the kitchen table. Told Jeffrey to go play. Then with her hand on her hips, she turned to him.

"What happened? Don't you realize that could have caught the house on fire? Ruin the sink? What were you thinking?"

"I could ask you the same questions."

She looked at him—confused. She looked at the sink, then to the garbage bag and then back at the sink.

"Don't tell me, you—a grown man read a child's diary and then you decided to burn it!"

"Yeah. That's exactly what happened."

"But why?"

"Why?" He stared adamantly. How could she play so innocent? Oh, but that was her role.

"Harvey, what is the matter with you?'

She played the role so well. "Who was he?" he asked frigid.

"Who was who?"

"Who picked the rose petals?"

The color drained from her face but only for a moment, then it was back.

"It was a long time ago. It didn't mean a thing. We were just kids. Kids who got carried away and didn't know what they were doing. It only happened that one time."

"You led me to believe that you were a virgin."

"No, I said I wouldn't have sex until I was married."

"It was a little late to be saying that, wasn't it. What's that old saying— why buy the cow when the milk is free. Or maybe this one worked better for your lover— shutting the barn door after the horse is out—or should I say whore!"

He thought she was going to slap him, but she didn't. She left the kitchen, went into their bedroom and shut the door. He followed her.

"Look, I'm sorry for what I said."

"Go away."

"I didn't mean that. You know I didn't"

"Just leave me alone."

"Mildred." She didn't answer. "I'm sorry. Ok?" Still she didn't reply. She sat on the bed, just staring into space. "You have no right to be mad at me. You're the one who lied. I want to know who it was." Still no answer. He stared at her for a second, then stormed out of the room, out of the house.

When he got to work at three thirty, he went to the break room. Kinkade was sitting at a table next to the drink machine. He dropped in a quarter then punched a button. He didn't think about how hard until Kinkade laughed.

"You got a personal beef with that drink machine?"

"No. But I do with Mildred." He sat his drink on the table, then straddled the chair. "How long have we known each other, Kinkade? What ten—maybe fifteen years?"

"I don't know, man. I guess. Why?"

"And you knew Mildred all your life—right."

"Yeah. Her parents and mine were friends. What's bugging you."

"I found out this afternoon that Mildred wasn't a virgin when we got married."

Kinkade looked down at his drink. His hands cupped the cold Pepsi can. "Look, man, that was a long time ago. It means nothing." He didn't look up.

"I should have been told back then."

"Yeah. I guess you're right. I didn't know if she told you or not. I knew it wasn't my place to mention it. You guys seemed to hit it off from the start. It meant nothing. It happened one time."

Kinkade lifted his eyes. Dark shameful eyes. "I don't know if I should say I'm sorry or what, but like I said it was just once—long before you two even met."

He heard his words—knew what they meant, but he didn't want to hear them. This was his best friend. His best friend crushed the rose petals that belonged to him. He could not say a word. He just looked at him. Kinkade continued as if explaining everything would make it alright.

"It was a Saturday afternoon. I went over for awhile. The night before there had been a party. She had just turned sixteen. I had promised her mom I would help clean up the mess from the party. There was no one there, her parents had gone somewhere—I don't know—to town— somewhere—we were alone.

"We were just horsing around. I grabbed her. We started out wrestling—one thing led to another—we were—it happened. She was so ashamed. She wouldn't speak to me for two months. Finally we talked. It was something we both wanted to forget. We were friends— not lovers. We were both embarrassed about it. I don't understand why she told you about it now."

He was not able to admit she didn't. This just made everything worse. He was supposed to be able to talk to his best friend about this wife who had done him wrong. He never would have thought the wrong was done with his best friend. They both had betrayed him.

"It's nothing," he said. "Time to go to work."

He got up from the table, walked into the mill, then out another door. He sat on the riverbank all afternoon. He didn't tell anyone he quit his job. The next morning he walked into the local newspaper office. He found out they needed someone to write the obituary page. He worked there for two weeks, never telling Mildred he had left the mill. Then one afternoon when he returned from work, she was waiting for him.

"Why didn't you tell me you left the mill?"

"Who told you?"

"Jill. She said Kinkade said you quit. No explanation. Just walked out. You want to explain this to me."

"There's nothing to explain. It was time to move on."

"And just when were you going to tell me about this 'move'?"

"I'm telling you now. I quit my job. I have another job. I work at the paper. You need anything else?"

She stared at him. He couldn't identify what the look meant. He didn't know if he had hurt her or if she was angry. He turned away, there was nothing left to be said.

He could never forgive her for the lie. They had three children together. Thirty years of marriage, but he never forgot. He never mentioned it again—but he never forgot. And he never trusted her again. If she was late, he wondered where she was. If she said she didn't want to have sex because her head hurt, he didn't believe her. If she spent thirty-five dollars on groceries, he always checked the checkbook, looked for receipts. Always looking—always checking. Never believing.

When she got sick and died, he welcomed it. It was over. Finished. He could put it all behind him.

He pulled into his driveway, turned off the switch. Now there was Mary Ellen. Gentle Mary Ellen. He knew Mary Ellen was a virgin. He could tell she knew nothing about a man. The way she kissed, touched him, so easy to blush—all of it said she was a virgin. He would finally have his virgin. Oh, there would be blood that night! Plenty of blood on their wedding night or he would know why not.

He smiled. Mary Ellen was the virgin he deserved years ago.

He got out of the car and walked into the house. He would give her a call later tonight. Let her know he was thinking of her—hear her tell him how much she was missing him. Oh yes, Mary Ellen would make him a fine acquiescence wife.

Chapter Seventeen

Mary Ellen eased out the back door. She had changed from her dress into a pair of jeans and a sweatshirt. A night breeze flipped her ponytail slightly. It was quiet out here, she needed that. Needed the fresh air to cleanse her mind and conscience. A heavy sigh eased from her. Oh, the confusion that rattled her brain.

David's kiss should have stirred no emotions within her! She wasn't some lovesick teenager any more. And how come she was finding herself wanting away from Harvey instead of with him? They were getting married in a few days. They should be together tonight. But she wanted to be alone.

And mother! Oh, that woman could drive a dead man out of his grave! She was driving her out of her mind! Why could she not leave it along about Harvey? Harvey wasn't a murderer.

She's sitting inside that house right now in front of the TV, drawing up crazy ideas about Harvey, just waiting for a chance to pounce him again.

Mary Ellen sat down on the back steps. She draped her arms around her legs, her chin resting on her knees.

There was no way Harvey killed his wife. He was a gentle, kind, loving man. Why would he kill her? Harvey said they had a good marriage. That Mildred was good at everything she did. She could have been anything she desired and he felt honored that such a wonderful creature would love him. He knew God had given her to him and he was grateful for the privilege of being her husband. How many times had he told her this? Competing with her would be hard...a perfection almost impossible to achieve.

Would he feel that way if something happened to her? Would she ever be able to fill Mildred's shoes? Mildred seemed so perfect. She had known her for only a few months before she died, and she seemed very nice. But Harvey made her sound like a saint.

There is no way he would harm her.

"Hey."

She jumped.

"Come here."

Her eyes strained into the darkness. The voice was coming from near the fence.

"Mary Ellen," the voice whispered.

"David?"

He giggled. He actually giggled. Just like he did when he was a kid and up to something.

"David, go away."

"No, not until you talk to me." His tone was now serious.

"I have nothing to say to you."

"Come on."

"You have caused me enough trouble. Just go away."

"Ah El, you know I never meant to cause you any trouble. Did Harvey find out about us?"

"There is no us. And no, he didn't."

"Ok. So talk to me."

"Will you just go away? I don't want to talk to you."

"Please. We've always been able to talk. I don't want to leave town like this."

"Why not? It didn't faze you fifteen years ago."

"Ah come on, El, let the past go and stop blaming me for being a kid. If you don't come over here and talk to me, I'm going around front and ring the doorbell. Your mom will let me in."

"Don't you dare!"

"Then come over here. Besides, if you don't I'll have to shout so you can hear me. You said you didn't want anyone to know about us."

"Stop saying that. There is 'no us'."

"Ok. If you won't come to me…" He put his hand upon the fence and hoisted himself upward. He was straddled over the pointed fence, balancing himself as he threw his other leg over. Mary Ellen jumped up from the porch.

"What do you think you're doing?" she demanded, her hands on her hips. She then marched down the steps, crossing the yard to David. She reached him just as he lost his balance and tumbled to the ground. With a sheepish grin he looked up at her.

"The fair lady to my rescue."

"The fair lady is going to kick your butt! David get up and go home."

"Not until we talk," he replied, standing and dusting off his pants. A smile boldly spread across his face. "So the fair lady is going to kick my butt, huh? That might be fun."

"David! You're impossible." She whirled around but

he caught her arm.

"El, you and I are friends. Regardless of what is going on right now, we are friends. I'm leaving in a few days. We must talk."

She looked into his eyes. They were still the warm eyes of childhood. The friend of long ago. Why did he leave? Why did he come back now?

"What is there to talk about, David. Like you said, in a few days you will leave and we haven't kept in touch all these years. I don't see what all the fuss is about."

"Because all these years I knew that skinny kid who lived next door was a friend…that the memories were nice. I don't want a memory of you being hurt—angry with me. It's not fair."

"And it's fair for you to come back here messing with my head."

"Ah, El, you know that wasn't what I was trying to do. Come on now—give me a chance to be friends. It's only fair."

"Oh, alright. But no more of this trying to kiss me or trying to pretend that there is an us when you know there never was."

"Promise." He caught her hand and pulled her to the stones that surrounded a small fishpond. "Remember the summer your dad built the pond?"

"How could I forget? We kept getting in the way by helping. You almost pushed him in when you ran the wheelbarrow into the pond. If there had been any fish in it then, you would have scared them to death."

He laughed. "Well, you weren't any help either. I think you were the one who put the fish in before he had the lining secure. All the fish had to be dipped back out."

She laughed with him. "It was fun, wasn't it. So easy— relaxed." They sat down on the rocks. "Are there fish in there now?"

"Oh, sure. Old Buster just died about five years ago."

"You're kidding! That fish lived over fifteen years! No way!"

She laughed. "Ok, I guess it has been a little longer then that."

David flipped the water. "Your mom always liked this pond. Where is she tonight?"

"Inside watching TV. You know how mom is." She hesitated. "No, you don't, do you? She hasn't been the same since dad died. She can come up with some of the craziest ideas. Right now she thinks Harvey is a wife killer."

"What!"

"You heard me right. She has drawn up this crazy notion that maybe he killed his first wife. That's why they moved here. So he could quietly kill her."

"She's not serious is she?"

"I don't know. Yeah—I think she is, if I'm honest."

He laughed.

"It's not funny."

"Yes it is. Think about it. Your mom thinks your future husband is a killer. Talk about an imagination running wild. You just aren't looking at this right."

"And just how am I supposed to be looking at it?"

"Your mom, the nice, mild mannered church going lady of the neighborhood has decided to play cops and killers and she's pulled your boyfriend into her game whether he likes it or not. And it's funny."

"I'm glad you think so. If you were sitting in my place

you would see no humor in it."

"Maybe. Might as well, though. She's going to do what she pleases."

"Would you believe she climbed into the dumpster looking for that pin the dropper sent here?"

He laughed. Then she laughed. "I guess it is kinda funny. Mom climbing into a dumpster. Only if dad could have seen her!" She snickered.

"Why was it in the dumpster?"

"Harvey threw it away and mom went looking for it."

"Threw it away! Don't he realize he shouldn't do that?"

"Yeah. Now he does. He's not going to throw anything else away..." Her voice dropped. "...if he threw it away."

"What?"

"Nothing. I need to get inside. It's getting late."

"OK. Friends?"

She smiled. "Friends." She stood up. David stood with her. Then he slipped his arm around her and gave her a big bear hug. "Take care of yourself."

"When are you leaving?"

"Early Saturday morning."

"Two days left for the big city of Farley to entertain you, huh?"

"Yeah. Not there's much here to entertain with." He caught her hand. "El, what do you think about us going over to Huntsville tomorrow night for dinner? Give us a chance to visit before I leave. How about it?"

"I don't know about that," she faltered. "I mean...Harvey...he will probably come over tomorrow evening...I don't think he would like it if I was out." She laughed half-heartedly. "Who am I kidding. He would have a fit if I went out to dinner with you. I can't blame him. I wouldn't like it if he went out with an old friend who buzzed into town. And neither would you."

"I guess you're right." He hesitated for a moment. "My fair lady," he said as he bowed at the waist. "May I please have the honor of a luncheon date at the mid-day hour of the new day that will be upon us when the sun is rising in the east?"

She laughed. He kissed her hand. He tilted his head in a downward movement, turned on his heel. His departing words spoken softly, "And until tomorrow, I will bid you farewell, my lady."

She couldn't help the laughter that spilled from her. It was a warm good-natured laughter that soothed her tired heart. She watched him as he climbed back over the fence. This time landing safely on the other side without tumbling to the ground. It reminded her of when they were kids and would sneak into one another's yards when they were supposed to be inside for the night. They laughed and teased each other, each one telling the other to be quiet and then have a case of the giggles where they couldn't stop. Such simple times.

Unknown to them, a door closed silently in the darkness. Listening ears slipped quietly into the night.

Chapter Eighteen

Mary Ellen eased back into the house and up the back stairs. She removed the ribbon from her hair, letting it fall softly around her shoulders. She pulled the shirt over her head, and then slipped out of her jeans. Going into the bathroom, she turned the knob to hot. The room filled with steam as she brushed her teeth. The phone was ringing, but she stepped into the tub. She didn't want to talk to Harvey. And she didn't want to think about David.

He would be gone by this time Saturday…gone out of her life forever. By the time he returned—five or ten years from now—she would be married and living on some quiet street of Farley. His wild adventure was in another world far far away. She wondered what it was like to live that way. Throw a few things in your bag and fly away. See countryside that was completely different than anything she had ever known. It had to be exciting.

The warm water washed over her body. Steam filled the room. She wondered what her mother had told Harvey—if it was him on the phone. Any other time she would have talked with him. But not tonight. She was tired. That was it…just tired.

She shouldn't be like this. It wasn't fair to Harvey. It wasn't his fault she was acting like a lost kid thinking about days long past.

A faint knock entered the room, but she didn't respond. It came again.

"Mary Ellen." Her mother stood on the other side of the bathroom door, knocking gently. "Mary Ellen."

"Yes, mother."

"That was Harvey on the phone. He wanted to speak with you. He said you had a headache. Are you ok?"

"Yes, ma'am."

"Do you need an aspirin?"

"No, ma'am."

"Can I get you anything? You don't normally get sick. Are you sure you're ok?"

"I'm fine."

"Do you want me to tell him you'll call him back?"

"No."

"Is everything ok?"

"Yes, mother. Everything is fine."

"Do you need…"

"No, mother I just need this hot shower. That's all."

"And you aren't calling him back?"

"Is he still on the line?"

"Yes."

"Then just tell him I will talk to him tomorrow. I need to rest tonight."

"What do I tell him about your headache?"

"It's better." Was that a lie? If you don't have a headache and then you say it's better is that a lie? "Mother…"

"Yes, Mary Ellen?"

"Just tell him my head is fine. I will call tomorrow. Tell him I am in the shower." At least that part wasn't a lie.

"Alright."

She heard her mother walk across the hardwood floor. She knew her mother just as well as she knew her own hand. Her mother would be smiling all the way down those stairs, just knowing she was going to tell Harvey he would have to wait to talk to her daughter.

Why? Why did she now seem as if she didn't want her to marry Harvey? She couldn't really believe Harvey killed his wife. If she thought that, why didn't she say something before—when he first asked her out. Come to think of—she never was that excited about it when Harvey asked her out. Was she afraid of losing her? Maybe that's what it was all about.

She turned off the water, stepped from the shower and grabbed a towel. She wrapped it around her head, then pulled another one out of the closet for her body. Quickly she dried herself, then the towel fell to the floor as she stepped into a long white terry cloth bathrobe. She left the bathroom, moving across the room to the dresser. She removed the towel and began blow drying her hair.

She thought she was alone until she felt the tap on her shoulder. She jumped, whirling around to face Gladys.

"Don't do that!"

"I didn't think you could hear me with that thing blowing. How come you're so jumpy any way? What's the matter with you? Why didn't you tell me you aren't feeling well? Harvey says you're sick. You've been up here all alone. You could have at least said something."

"It was a headache, mother. Not a death watch. I'm fine."

"I told him you would call tomorrow. That seemed to satisfy him." She turned to leave, but stopped. As if she just couldn't let it go, she turned back to Mary Ellen. She looked at her for a moment. Just looking at her.

"What?"

"You. Something's not right here."

"What are you talking about? Honestly, Mother, you need to quit watching so much TV. Nothing is quiet right with you."

"I can sense things. I can tell when things just don't add up. And that headache, missy, just doesn't stack."

Mary Ellen turned on her blow drier. She flipped her hair as the warm air swirled around her head. She ran her fingers through her hair, shaking it, crunching it, working her fingers through the wet strands. She wanted her mother to leave the room. Stop staring at her. If she would just leave the room, if she just didn't have to make eye contact. Oh, God, please don't let her know about David. Now she was beginning to sound like David! What was there to know? They talked. That's all they did. Talk.

No, one. No one knew about the emotions he stirred within her. No one could read her mind. She couldn't even read her own mind—she never knew what she would be thinking from one minute to the next!

"Mary Ellen! Turn that darn thing off! I'm talking to you."

She flipped the switch. She turned around and faced Gladys.

"Ok, talk."

"I want to know what is going on?"

"Nothing is going on. I'm drying my hair."

"Don't you get sassy with me. You know darn well what I'm talking about. Two weeks ago you couldn't keep yourself away from Harvey Broyhill. Tonight you have a headache. Tonight you're in the shower when he calls. I've seen you almost break your neck to get to the phone. I want to know what's going on."

Then Gladys squinted her eyes, tilted her head slightly. "Have you decided maybe I was right?"

"Right? Of course not!"

"I don't know about that. Something sure has changed your tune tonight." She looked at her as if she had placed her under a microscope—turning, probing, searching. "And I think I know what it is."

"It's nothing. Nothing has changed. I had a headache—a severe headache. I took three extra-strength aspirins for it. That should tell you just how bad it was."

"Bad, huh? Yeah. Ok."

"What's that supposed to mean?"

Gladys shrugged her shoulders. "Why, nothing." She turned around and moved toward the doorway.

"It was bad," Mary Ellen defended.

"Yes, dear, I'm sure it was." Gladys tossed the words over her shoulders.

"Well..." She started to declare again just how horrible her head had been hurting, then Gladys reminded her of her dad's favorite saying. A kicked dog hollers. Who was it that said, 'I think ye protest too much.' Shakespeare?

She flipped the drier on. The buzzing drowned out anything her mother may have added—if anything. She wondered what she meant? She was afraid to ask. The last thing she needed was for her mother to think there was something going on with David.

Oh, she should have never promised to go to lunch with him. Her mother will know...and she'll break her neck to tell Harvey. She should have just made plans to meet him somewhere.

She stopped. Stared at herself in the mirror. What kind of woman was she becoming? Lying. Sneaking around with another man. Ok, so it was just David, but David was so different from Harvey. David was smooth, cool, handsome. David was the kind of man the women noticed when he walked down the street. Nice shoulders, nice flat stomach. Nice arms. Beautiful smile. Perfect teeth. Prettiest eyes a girl could look into.

Oh, Mary Ellen, she moaned, would you please shut up! Guilt swept over her.

She tossed the dryer onto the dresser. Flipping back the comforter, she curled up in the bed with damp hair. It would be a long night.

Chapter Nineteen

When she opened the kitchen door the next morning, she wouldn't believe her eyes. There was flour all over the kitchen. On the counter—on the floor—everywhere. Her mother stood at the counter with her back to Mary Ellen. Mary Ellen stood at the bottom of the kitchen stairs.

"What in the world are you doing?"

"Oh, good morning, baby."

"I'm not cleaning up this mess."

Gladys turned to look at her daughter. There was also flour on Gladys' face. "That's ok, baby. I will."

She couldn't believe her ears. Ten years she had not come near this kitchen except to eat and now this morning she has decided to turn it upside down and strewing flour all over it. What was going on with her!

"What are you doing?"

"Rolls. Remember when you were a little girl I used to make rolls?"

"I don't remember there being flour all over the kitchen."

"Oh, so I spilled a little. No big deal."

"Why are you making rolls?"

"I just thought it would be nice. I love the smell of yeast rolls." She turned back to her batter. "Don't you?"

"What?"

"Like the smell of yeast rolls."

Mary Ellen eased on into the kitchen. "Yeah...they're fine...have you been outside this morning?" Her eyes glanced at the clock over the sink. Seven. She didn't mean to sleep that late. It had been almost three when she finally dozed off. Her eyes felt heavy and raw as if no sleep had touched them for days.

Gladys turned to face her. "No. I haven't looked to see if there was a rose. I thought you should. It's what eight—nine days until your day?"

"Nine."

"That's right. Today's Thursday." She turned back to her dough. "Wasn't that a nice sermon last night?"

Sermon? She didn't know. She was in the nursery. Wouldn't have mattered though. All she could think about was that pin on Gloria's sweater. Her pin on Gloria! How could Harvey do that? He didn't want her to have it, yet he gave it to his daughter. She didn't know if she was mad or hurt. Maybe both. Oh if mother knew about that...

She mumbled a low moan as she walked around the flour and through the dining room door. She wanted to see if there was anything on the front steps.

If it had been there all night—been there long enough to have the morning frost, maybe it would give her an idea of when it was placed. Who was doing this, knew her routine. Knew when it was safe to leave the rose, leaving it just long enough to be found safely. Long enough to destroy her life. That's what it was doing. It was destroying her. If not for those stupid roses she would be going out for last minute items for her wedding with joy.

Today she needed to double check the caterer to make

sure everything was ready. Today was the day she also set aside to pick up Harvey's ring. She had ordered it the week after he had proposed. They had told her it would come in this week. She had not even checked to see if it was in. In all the chaos that had been going on she had forgotten about it. Until now.

She eased opened the front door. It would be there. She could just feel it. The soft yellow rose was laying there in all its beauty on the sandstone step. Such beauty, yet it brought such sorrow.

The morning sun touched it. There was no morning frost. Only light dew that the warm sun was drying. Mary Ellen bent down, picked it up, and touched it to her nose. The petals were as soft as velvet, the fragrance as gentle as warm sunshine.

Who was doing this? And why? Why now?

She turned to go back into the house but stopped. She stared at the small red sport car sitting in the drive next door. Was it possible? Would David do this to her? Would he out of his own hurt not want her to find happiness after all these years? When did he come to town? When did he get divorced? Did he know she was getting married that day he picked her up?

Her mind tried to think back. How long ago was it when he came cruising down the street in his new sport car. What did he say about her marriage? In all the turmoil, she couldn't remember.

She looked at the rose then back at the car. Surely not. But still.

"Mary Ellen." She turned. Her mother was standing in the doorway. Her eyes went to the rose. "I see it's here again." She held open the big screen door. "You have a phone call."

"It is Harvey?"

"No. It's David."

"David? What does he want?" She could feel the annoyance building. She didn't really think he sent the roses, yet her subconscious was angry with him. Maybe her subconscious knew more then she wanted to admit.

"I don't know what he wants. I learned a long time ago, if they don't tell you, they probably don't want you to know."

"Well, that never stopped you from asking Harvey."

"That's different."

"How's that different?"

"Because he murdered his wife."

"Stop saying that!"

"Did I tell you I have Nathan working on some things for me?"

"No, you didn't! What things?"

"Come on inside. There's no point in discussing this out here. And besides you need to see what David wants. He such a nice boy."

"Nice, huh, nice. Well maybe he's the one sending these roses, have you ever thought about that?"

"Of course not. And don't be saying anything so foolish out here in the yard. Someone might hear you. Get in the house if you're going to talk foolishness. See what the boy wants."

She threw the rose in the trash basket beside the big chair as she reached for the phone.

"Yes."

"Good morning, my Fair Lady."

"What do you want, David?" Her voice was distant. .

Her tone put him off for a second. "You ok this morning, El?"

"Sure. Why wouldn't I be? I got my morning rose."

"I'm sorry, hon."

"Are you?"

"What do you mean? Sure I am. I know how this has been tearing you apart."

"David, if I asked you something, you would tell me the truth, wouldn't you?"

"Of course."

"Is it you?"

"You've got to be kidding, El! How could you think I would be the one behind such? You know I wouldn't do that."

"It's not you?"

"NO!" His voice rushed into her ear loud and clear. "What kind of question is that?"

"I had to ask, David. You came home. I'm getting roses..."

"Think for a moment, Mary Ellen. You were getting roses before I got here. I'll let you go."

"David, I'm sorry. I just had to ask."

"You shouldn't have. You should have known. I've got to go."

"But what did you call about?"

"Lunch. But I think it's best we don't have lunch. Best I get packed."

"Wait, David. Give me a chance."

"I'll see you, Mary Ellen." He hung up.

She stared into the black receiver. He called her Mary Ellen. He never called her Mary Ellen.

. Gladys was standing behind her. When she turned, she

almost bumped into her. "Just had to ask the one person you knew wouldn't be guilty, didn't you? Do you realize you have been suspicious of everyone you know? Why not accuse the preacher. How about the head deacon. Or maybe Alice Petrie."

"Just shut up, mother, just shut up." She slammed the receiver down and rushed from the room. She went through the kitchen, ran straight through the flour on the floor and up the back stairs.

Gladys sat down in the big chair. She had flour on her nose, her cheek, but she didn't care. Her life had always been quiet and peaceful—maybe a little too peaceful sometimes. She never really did have an adventurous spirit after she and Norbert married. She just saw life as home, family, and church.

But once Norbert was gone, it was as if everything was over. Sure, she still had Mary Ellen. But she always thought Mary Ellen would have been married before now. She never thought about it just being the two of them for ten years.

She had not told Mary Ellen her plans. She was waiting. It was important that she wait. She had once visualized Mary Ellen marrying a fine young man, upstanding in the community, maybe a doctor—at least someone with a fine job. And there would be grandbabies. Lots of grandbabies. She never let Mary Ellen know she was an only child because she couldn't have any more children. She didn't want to admit that to anyone. She never even told Norbert. It made her a failure—at least in her eyes.

Her mother had four kids—raised six—two belonging to an out-of-state sister of her mother's that no one ever met. Six kids and all she could have was one. Her mother was eighty-five years old now. And acted just like she was forty-five. Did anything and everything and for the last ten years, she, Gladys had lived her life as a dead woman.

But those roses. They had put a spark back into her life. It was a mystery. It was an adventure. But it was tearing Mary Ellen apart. And Harvey. Even he had become a mystery. Just where did he come from?

The phone rang, jerking her away from all the questions that flooded her mind. "Hello," she said.

"I could find no record of Harvey Broyhill in Denver, Colorado. Are you sure that's where he's from?" Nathan asked.

"I knew he was lying. Yes. Denver. He always talked about working for a newspaper in Denver. He murdered his wife. He came here to this one horse-town because he knew he could get away with it. How on earth that sweet daughter of his could not see what he has done to her mother…"

"Now hold on, Gladys. You're getting ahead of yourself."

"But you just said you could not find any record of him in Denver. What more do you need to know to prove this man is hiding something. I've got to tell Mary Ellen."

"No, don't."

"Why not."

"If you do, she will tell Harvey and he will know you're—I'm—checking on him. We don't need that.'

"Alright. I guess you're right. What are you going to do next?"

"I've got a few ideas. You're sure about where he came from?"

"That's what he said. Maybe I need to say something to Mary Ellen."

"No. Just hold off until later in the day. I'm going to check a few things."

"Alright, but I don't like this."

"I know. But you don't say a word. What about Mary Ellen? Was there a rose this morning?"

"Oh yes. Just like before. She threw it in the trash." She wasn't able to tell him about the accusations she threw at David. David was a nice boy. He wouldn't do something like this. There would be no reason for him to do this. There was never anything but friendship between the two of them.

Besides, this person, whoever it is, has to be twisted, kooky or something. If they didn't want Mary Ellen to get married, why not just ask her out. Lord knows she's been sitting home long enough for him to have already asked.

Mary Ellen sure wasn't having much luck with men, come to think about it. Some kook sending roses and a fiancé who's a wife killer. She should have nipped it all in the bud when she saw it coming. Nipped it in the bud! Hum—that was a good one.

"Gladys, Gladys, did you hear me?"

"What? Sure I heard you. You said for me to keep my mouth shut."

"Yes. But I also said I would call you tonight. Were you going to be home?"

"Home?" Sure she would be home. Where would she be going? Unless…

"What time?"

"Around seven…there about."

"Make it nine."

"Nine? Well, ok. Nine."

"Hold on, Nathan, the front bell is buzzing like crazy. I don't know who it would be this early."

"Maybe there's another package…"

Chapter Twenty

Loud bangs were coming from the front door. Gladys hurried toward the door. She jerked opened the door.

"David!"

"Where is she?"

"Mary Ellen? She's upstairs." He stormed up the stairs two at a time. "First door to your left!" she called after him. Gladys rushed back to the phone. "Nathan, I'll have to talk with you later."

"Something wrong?"

She sniggered "I hope so."

"What?"

"Nothing. Talk to you later." Before he could protest farther, she hung up the phone and charged the stairs.

At the top, she slowed. She didn't want Mary Ellen to know she was near. This should be good.

David had reached the top of the stairs. He boiled down the hallway, slung open the bedroom door. Mary Ellen lay across the bed. She jumped when the door hit the wall. Quickly she rolled over, stared at David.

"What are you doing barging in here, banging doors?"

He crossed the room in three swift steps. "Just who do you think you are accusing me of sneaking roses to you? Just what kind of man do you think I am?" he threw the questions to her.

Mary Ellen rose from the bed. "Look, David, I said I was sorry. You hung up before I had a chance to really apologize. But think how you would feel if I had showed up in your town, and you were suddenly getting roses."

"I didn't just show up. Mom had been trying to get me to come down ever since the divorce. Just because I show up now—as you put it—gives you no right to accuse me of anything. And another thing—if I wanted to send flowers, I think I know how without offending anyone. I don't have to sneak around if I am interested in a woman.

"And what makes you think I want to send you flowers in the first place!"

Oh, that one stung! He's hot, Gladys decided. She stood out of sight next to the doorway. She was waiting for Mary Ellen's comeback.

"David, I—I just—well…"

That was weak.

"You just what?" Mary Ellen hesitated. "Yeah, that's what I thought," David said.

"Can you not forgive me? I was wrong."

"I already knew you were wrong. You're going to have to do better than that."

"What?"

He walked across the floor in two steps, grabbed her shoulders with both hands, his eyes bored into hers. "Tell me you won't ever doubt me again."

"What?"

"You heard me. Say it. 'David, I won't ever doubt you again.'"

"David, I won't ever doubt you again."

"Alright. Now it's settled. Don't ever forget those

words. Never." He let go of her shoulders, turned as if to leave. "I'll see you at twelve-thirty. Be over in that little red sport car at twelve-thirty. That way you can tell your Harvey I didn't pick you up for a date." He threw the words back at her.

Then he turned back to face her. He cupped her face in his hands. His lips touched hers lightly. "You owed me that one," he said as he walked from the room.

"Owe you!" Mary Ellen shouted. "Owe you!" But her fingers touched her lips.

He passed Gladys in the hallway. "Good morning, Mrs. Forsman," he said in a soft gentle voice.

He went down the stairs and out the front door. Gladys leaned over the banister watching him leave. He closed the front door quietly behind him. She flew down the stairs.

"David Petrie," she called as she jerked open the door. "Get yourself back here this very second!"

David turned, smiled. "Yes, Mrs. Forsman, what can I do for you?"

"You can tell me what's going on."

He smiled again. "Nothing. Just two old friends having lunch together. That's all."

"And the kiss?"

"What kiss? Was there a kiss?" He smiled mischievously. "You'll have to ask El about that." He got in his little red sport car and left.

Alice Petrie watched her son's car until he turned left at the end of the block. She stood on her front porch, bonnet on her head, pail and flower shovel in hand. She walked down the steps toward Gladys.

"Gladys," she called, "is there something wrong?"

"No. Everything is fine." Gladys stood on the sandstone step where just a short time earlier, Mary Ellen had picked up the yellow rose. She, too, had been watching David leave, but she didn't want Alice Petrie to know that. She adored David, but it seemed as if she and Alice Petrie were never on the same page. Almost as if they were competing with each other.

Even when the kids were little, the fathers got along fine, but Alice always thought she had the best of everything. If the kids had been making mud pies, according to Alice's philosophy, David's would have been better. That had been so long ago when things were simpler. Now, today, Gladys watched as Alice moved down her steps, crossed the yard.

"Did David say where he was going? I noticed he came from your house," Alice said as she reached the fence that divided the yards

She could have told her no, that he only came by to kiss her daughter. Instead she politely answered—at least politely for Gladys.

"No." Bluntly. Right to the point. No frills of how you're doing, or beautiful spring morning. Just a curt no, but at least there were no insults.

"He's leaving, you know."

Leaving? No, she didn't know. No one had bothered to tell her. Of course no one ever bothers to tell her anything. Why didn't Mary Ellen inform her of this news? Did Mary Ellen know? Surely she did.

Gladys moved down her steps slowly as if she were stalking game that she did not want to spook. Her gait was buoyant—easy causal steps. She spoke melodiously as if coaching a wild deer to take food from her hand.

"Where is he going?" She waited. One question at a time.

"Africa."

Oh, my land! Half-way around the world!

Steady—steady old girl. It's nothing to you if he moves to Tim Buck Two.

"When is he leaving?"

"In just a few days. He says he won't be here for the wedding. I so hoped he would be. They have been friends for so long. It would be a shame if he missed it."

Yes—just like it was a shame Mary Ellen wasn't invited to his. Of course it was out of town, but she could have gone with Alice and Ben. The parents of the groom should have been allowed to bring an old friend.

Maybe the bride was afraid of that old friendship, just like Harvey is. Harvey couldn't stand the idea of Mary Ellen near David. He would blow a fuse when he finds out about this lunch date.

Darn! She couldn't tell it! She wasn't supposed to know herself. Maybe Mary Ellen will let it slip before she leaves. If not...well...she would have to think of something. It was just too good not to let Harvey in on it. She smiled.

"What are you smiling about?"

"Oh, just thinking—really nothing. But back to David...you say he's leaving in a few days. Any way he could postpone it?"

"I don't think so. I noticed this morning he had packed. I thought he might even leave sooner than anticipated. But who knows. These single men move when they feel like it. You remember how it is. Oh, that's right...Mary Ellen has never left home, has she? Well I guess marriage will be good for her. Give her a chance to see the world."

See the world? They were moving across town. Not across the country. Oh , no! Harvey hasn't said something about leaving town with her baby? Not another small town. Another murder.

Her voice held its steady tone, but her stomach churned. "They aren't leaving town. Just a few blocks away."

"Really. I thought perhaps they might move back...where is it he's from...don't he have sons there. What's the name of that place now?"

"Denver."

"Denver, Colorado? Are you sure? I thought Mildred said something else...but maybe it was Denver...it was Den...something. I don't really remember. That has been a while."

The question. That all important question. Deep breath. Steady.

"What made you think they might move back from where he came? Gloria lives here now too."

"Yes, she does, but well, you know how people talk." No, tell me, Gladys thought as she waited for Alice to continue. "I heard some one saying Gloria was thinking about going home. She missed her old friends. Her husband's family is there also. But like I said you know how rumors get started."

There was no way Harvey was leaving Farley with her baby. She would stop him at any cost. Heck! The whole town thought she was crazy anyway and when it came to Mary Ellen, maybe she was. But she would never allow him to leave town with her baby. Mary Ellen would not become another ailing wife unto death.

"I guess she's all excited about the wedding. Mary Ellen is such a sweet child. Always has been. She was always one of my favorites of David's friends. David always had such a large group of friends—but none sweeter than Mary Ellen."

"Yes...yes..."

"Harvey seems like a nice man. I guess she couldn't have gotten a nicer man here in Farley. Mildred was always so nice."

"Yes...yes..."

Harvey was nice. Mildred was nice. Harvey was marrying her daughter. And Mildred was dead. Harvey—the man from Denver, who wasn't from Denver. The man who moves to a small town and his wife dies less then a year later.

Who was Harvey? Where did he come from? Why did his wife really die? All these questions stormed her brain and the wedding was in nine days. Today was Thursday. One week from this Saturday Mary Ellen would become the new Mrs. Harvey Broyhill. Oh, Mary Ellen! What are you doing?

"Oh, look, it looks like you're getting a package."

Gladys turned. There he was once again. The same delivery man walking up her steps. Why didn't Nathan go to that place and find out who is sending gifts? If he didn't, she would.

She rushed the man. He jumped as if he thought he was being attacked.

"Give me that," she demanded.

"What is it?" Alice cried. She leaned over the white picket fence, looking at Gladys and the delivery man.

"What's going on?"

"Nothing." Gladys said as she ripped the brown wrapping paper from the small package. Inside was a small brown box. She tugged at the tape that sealed the flaps. Inside the box was another box. Gently she lifted it, letting the brown cardboard box fall to the ground. *Estee Lauder* perfumes lay in the box. Not one, but three bottles. A note lay on top of the bottles.

Use your intuition for pleasures because you are so beautiful.
Nine days.

Gladys looked closely at the fragrances' names. Intuition. Pleasures. And Beautiful. Whoever he is, he has a good imagination.

"Gladys. Gladys," Alice called. "What's in the box? Is it a gift for Mary Ellen's wedding?"

"No," Gladys replied as she turned toward the house. Mary Ellen would not be wearing this to her wedding. Too bad she would throw it in the garbage. Best thing she could do was call Nathan and get him over here—fast.

"You left the box on your yard, Gladys. Trash on your lawn ruins the looks of your house," Alice informed.

"Nosey neighbors ruin the neighborhood," Gladys mumbled under her breath, but Alice didn't hear her.

Chapter Twenty One

Alice thought about picking up the box for Gladys, but decided against it as she watched Gladys close the front door. She could have at least revealed what was in the box. That would have been the polite thing to do. Maybe there is more here than she wants revealed. Alice smiled.

"Mary Ellen," Gladys called up the stairs. "You have another package."

"And why am I not surprised," retorted Mary Ellen as she came out of her bedroom and stood at the top of the stairs. "Just throw it into the trash."

"No, we can't do that. I'm calling Nathan and telling him to get his self over here—now."

Mary Ellen moved down the stairs. "Mother, if I didn't know you better, I would believe you have an interest in this Nathan. He's too young for you, you know that, don't you?"

"Don't talk such foolish talk. I'm old enough to be his—well never mind that—I know my age. This is police work and that's all."

Mary Ellen laughed as she reached the bottom of the stairs. "I do believe I have made my mother blush. Isn't that a switch?"

"I don't know what's got in to you, but this much I do know, you have a package here and another note. He is counting off your wedding days. I believe he will be at your wedding."

"Don't be absurd! He wouldn't dare show himself at the wedding. He's a coward. Why else would he be sending gifts and refusing to reveal who he is?"

"Do you want to see this?"

"No. I have no desire to see anything that is sent here by that horrible person."

"Perfumes," Gladys replied, ignoring Mary Ellen's wishes. She sprayed one of them on her hand, then sniffed her hand. "Umm. Smells good. Whoever he is, he has good taste. Good candy, pretty jewelry, now nice smelling perfumes.

"Mary Ellen, you are a pretty girl—and I'm not saying this just because I am your mother—but think about this. Not until you met Harvey have there been any boyfriends knocking on your door. Personally I think it's because you have always been so distant to people—kinda cool to folks—and that's why there never were young men on your doorsteps. But that's neither here nor there.

"But could it be that since you have Harvey that one of the young men in our church thinks it's a mistake for you to marry him and this is his way of breaking you two up?"

"That doesn't make any sense. Why would they care who I married? They never have bothered to approach me in the past."

"In the past you were always there. Now you won't be."

"No—no, it couldn't be. Who? All the men I know are either married, or have girlfriends. No. It has to be…"

"What?"

"I don't know." She looked at her mother with worried eyes. "I don't have the slightest idea who would do this." She walked past the box. "Call your officer."

She went to the piano and began to play as if nothing was wrong. Gladys went into the kitchen and picked up the wall phone. She dialed the number she now knew by heart.

Nathan picked up the box from the lawn as he walked up the walk. This was beginning to be a habit—him picking up Gladys' lawn.

Alice was working in her flowerbed by the fence. She watched Nathan through the fence. When he bent over, she stood up.

"I guess you're here about that package, huh?"

"What?" Nathan turned to face her.

"Let me introduce myself. My name is Alice Petrie. I am Gladys' Sunday School teacher. Been teaching over thirty years. You go to church? I don't believe I know your name. You from around here?" Her questions was as fast as any firing range bullets.

"Officer Nathan Oneal. It's nice to meet you, Mrs. Petrie. And yes, I am here about the package and the roses. Have you noticed anyone coming around here leaving anything?"

"Haven't looked, but if you like, I'll be glad to keep an eye on the place. Gladys, bless her heart, kinda keeps her head in the clouds, stays in a lot. But anything I can do to help, I'll be glad to."

"Good. Good."

Nathan approached the steps. The front door swung open. Gladys motioned him inside the house.

"I think you should call for a full-scale investigation.'

"I can't do that. Gladys, you watch too much TV. And I hate to tell you this—but I can't have any investigation."

"What are you talking about? Why not?"

"There has not really been a crime here."

"How can you say that?"

"Gladys, your daughter is getting gifts. Nothing but flowers and gifts. No threatening notes—"

"But there was a note. See. Here it is."

Gladys shoved the note at him. Nathan read the note carefully.

"But it's not a threatening note. It's really a compliment."

"But it's from him—the dropper—you can't be serious that it isn't a crime."

"It's not."

"Why haven't you said something before now?"

"I kept hoping he would make a slip-up and we would get him. But I can't come running over here every time because there isn't a crime. I have other things to work on."

"Oh, really," Gladys replied, throwing her hands upon her hips. "And I guess Farley is in a crime wave and your hands are full of murderers and thieves—what else—drug kings?"

"Mother, leave him alone." Mary Ellen had left her piano and came into the foyer. "Does it really matter any longer who it is? What harm can roses and gifts causes?"

"Mary Ellen, you have lost your mind. What are you thinking? Two days ago you were raving about this person out to destroy you and now you just calmly say leave it alone. I won't. Do you hear me? I won't."

"Really you have no choice. In nine days I will marry Harvey and life will be back to normal. David will go to Africa and Harvey and I will live on the other side of town. Things will be back to normal." Then pity touched her eyes as she stared into her mother's. "Except for you. You will be all alone in this big house. Just you."

"No," Gladys rebuked. "No. That will never happen." She turned to Nathan. "Tell her. Tell her what you found out about Harvey."

"Gladys, are you sure?"

"Tell her!"

"But, Gladys…"

"Tell her, darn it, tell her." She turned to Mary Ellen. "He lied to you." She looked back at Nathan. "Don't just stand there—tell her!"

"He's not from Denver."

"Alright." Mary Ellen waited for the next statement. Nothing else was said. "Is that it?"

"Is that not enough? You don't even know where this man is from. You don't even know what his past is, why he came here. Think about it, Mary Ellen. He came here and within one year his wife is dead."

"From cancer, mother, cancer. Not some poison as you have drawn up in your head. Don't you see what you are doing? You don't want me to marry Harvey and you are doing all this to stop it. Maybe even leaving roses to make Harvey jealous."

"No, no," she rebuked. "Never would I do such. It's not me. It's someone who loves you and sees the horror of Harvey."

Mary Ellen sighed heavily. "Oh, mother," she moaned

as she turned away.

"No. It's not that way." The phone was ringing. Mary Ellen moved to answer the phone. "Mary Ellen, listen to me. I swear it's not that way. I swear." She turned to Nathan. "You believe me don't you?"

He did, but he didn't know if he should tell her or not. Gladys had decided this so-called crime had to be solved and now that Mary Ellen decided she was the guilty party, Gladys would just be that much more determined.

The panic left her voice, left her face. "Alright. If you don't believe me, fine. I'll do it myself. I'll find this person. All I have to do is wait on him. That's all. And when I do, I'm going to shoot him!"

"You can't do that!"

"Oh, yes I can. I'll shoot him for trespassing."

"You can't shoot someone for trespassing."

"Well, you just watch me. What's that saying—'you just hide and watch'. I'll show you how it's done."

"Gladys, I am informing you right now, that it is against the law and you can not, I repeat, can not do this."

She smiled. "Give me that box of perfumes. Since you can't use it against the stalker, I'll use it myself."

"But he isn't stalking her. He's leaving gifts. He is what would be referred to as a secret admirer."

"How come you are changing your tune in the midst of all this? You were all for helping me and now it's a complete new game plan."

"I still want to help you. I'd like to know who this guy is too, but I can't help you when I am working."

Gladys' tone softened. "And when you aren't working?"

"We'll see."

Gladys smiled. "In that case, should we check for finger prints on the perfume?"

"We could, but I don't expect that's going to be our answer. If there is no record of his prints in the system, then it would be worthless. Tonight, we wait again. But this time, you don't get to go to bed. If I'm going to lose sleep, then so are you."

"Ok. Ok. You don't have to be so grumpy about it," Gladys replied.

"And where were you going tonight?" Nathan asked. Gladys smiled. "You aren't going to another dumpster, are you?" Gladys smiled again.

In the kitchen, Mary Ellen was speaking softly into the phone. She did not want her mother to hear. Harvey was calling about her headache. She told him she was fine this morning. That it eased off once she fell asleep. Lies were coming so easy now. It was true. Once the lies started, there was no end. And they rolled off easier each time.

"I think it would be good if you came over for dinner. Yes, about six."

"I guess you got another rose last night?" He wanted to hear a clear no. But his fear was a yes. She answered his fear. The rose was there.

"Any gifts yet?"

"Perfumes. Mother has them."

"What kind?"

"I don't know. I didn't pay any attention. Why?"

"Just wondering." He wondered how expensive they were. The pin was pretty—too pretty to toss in the trash. Gloria loved it. It was strange how he hated the idea of Mary Ellen having the pin, but found pleasure in giving it to Gloria. Gloria told him how sweet he was for giving her the pin. She didn't know someone else had bought it…bought it for his future wife. Little details that weren't important since they did not touch Gloria's life. Mary Ellen would never know.

In nine days they would be married and it would not matter what Mary Ellen knew or thought. She would belong to him and he would tell her what she should think and feel. She would not be another Mildred. He would never have another Mildred in his life. Mildred should have been eliminated from his life long ago, but he wouldn't look back on the past. The only thing that mattered was Mary Ellen being the wife he desired.

"What are your plans for today?" he asked her.

She could not tell him about David. This was the perfect opportunity to tell him, but she couldn't get the words past her lips. Instead she responded, "Piano lessons. I have four students this afternoon."

"And this morning?"

"My own lessons. I must practice for church. I must be ready for Sunday." She didn't mention David. Her mother didn't know about David. Harvey would never know. If she told him, he would get angry. He would insist she didn't go. She wanted to spend the time with David before he left. Once she was married, once he was gone, never again would there be a day like today. She had to keep the date—no—it wasn't a date. It was two old friends going for lunch. Nothing more.

Always that piano, thought Harvey. Once they were married, that piano would not be taking her time away from him. She would have to manage her time so it did not interfere with her duties to him.

He may let her still have her students after the

marriage though. It would be extra money coming into the budget. He didn't know about her playing for the church. There was no money there. She refused to even suggest being paid. Of course, it would be good socially—his wife the church pianist. But still he didn't know about the time involved.

Her time would be his time and he did not want to compete with anyone or anything for her time. Mary Ellen would make the perfect wife. He could mold her and shape her just as he pleased.

"I will be there around six. I want those perfumes thrown out."

"Mother would never allow that!"

"You don't answer to your mother. I am your husband to be. You don't belong to your mother. You belong to me."

He sounded so strong and powerful when he used that tone. There was a time when her knees would have gone weak, but today she was torn. Her loyalty to her mother or for her future husband. Why was she always caught in the middle?

"Nathan is here."

"What's he doing there?"

"Mother called him when the package came. She may give the perfumes to him."

He didn't like the sound to that. He didn't like the police always around. Always snooping. He detested them. "How long has he been there?" Was Gladys trying to match her daughter with the young officer? "Tell her you don't need the police over there every time you turn around."

He's the one who suggested they call the police in the

beginning. What was wrong with him? wondered Mary Ellen.

"Mary Ellen," Gladys said as she came through the kitchen door, "I'm going out for awhile. Is that Harvey? I want to talk to him."

"No, mother."

"What is she talking about? What does she want?"

"I need to tell him something."

"Mary Ellen, what does you mother want?"

"Nothing."

"Harvey," Gladys shouted, "I know you lied. I'm going to prove it too."

"Lied? Mary Ellen, what is going on?"

"Nothing." She put her hand over the mouthpiece. "Mother, will you get out of here. If I didn't know better, I would swear you were drinking. What's got into you yelling at him like that? Where's Nathan? Go talk to your cop friend. Get out of here."

"Did you tell him we know he's not from Denver? Did you ask yourself why he lied about where he came from? I'm telling you there is plenty going on here. Plenty! Best thing for you is to find out who you're marrying."

"Mother, please," Mary Ellen said, her hand still over the mouthpiece. She turned her back to her mother, turned her attention to Harvey. "Let me let you go. I'll see you tonight."

"Mary Ellen, what is that woman talking about? What lie? Has she lost her mind? Mary Ellen, she just don't want you to get married. You can't listen to her."

"I know—I know. I'll talk with you tonight."

She hung up the receiver before he could object. She then turned on her heel in pursuit of Gladys.

"How could you do that?" she demanded. She caught up with Gladys at the foot of the stairs. Gladys had one foot on the bottom step as to go up stairs, then she changed her mind and grabbed her sweater from the coat tree.

"How could I do what?"

"Don't play innocent with me. You know what I'm talking about. What lie?"

"He's not from Denver."

"So. Who cares?"

"You should. I'm going out."

"Where?"

"Why should you care? You don't care that you're marrying a liar and a murderer."

She could have screamed, but she didn't. She wasn't sure she could stop if she began. Instead, she stomped up the stairs, and Gladys slammed the front door as she departed. Today would be the day she carried out her plan. She would wait no longer.

Chapter Twenty Two

The sun was shining bold and bright when Mary Ellen walked out of her house. She stopped on the porch for a few seconds. Her eyes scanned across the yard. There was no one in sight. Mrs. Petrie had gone inside or else around back. David stood beside his car. He caught her eye, and gave her a big wave. She went down the steps slowly.

It was twelve thirty. Harvey was on his lunch break, seated in the cafeteria at the paper, eating his turkey sandwich. She knew he was eating a turkey sandwich because it was Thursday. On Thursdays he always had a turkey sandwich. On Friday he ate fish. It had nothing to do with his religious upbringing. Friday was the day he ate fish. Fish sticks and little green peas that he warmed in the microwave.

She wondered where she and David would go for lunch. Was it a sin to go to lunch with an old friend and not tell your future husband? Two weeks ago she would have not gone. Two weeks ago she told Harvey everything.

"Your chariot awaits, My Lady," David said as he opened the car door for her.

"And where are we going?"

"It's a surprise. You are not allowed to ask any

questions. When we arrive, then you can ask all the questions you want."

"Alright." She readily agreed. Perhaps they would go outside Farley to a neighboring town. That would be good. She suddenly became aware of the fact she did not want anyone to see them. She didn't want to be peppered with Harvey's questions. If he asked too many questions, would her lips say one thing and her eyes reveal another? Was she being honest even with herself?

No matter. In a few days David would be gone. And he would never come again into her life. There would never be another lunch like this one today. Today was the lunch she longed for twenty years ago.

They rode in silence. The sun sent a warm breeze onto her face as he lowered the top of the car. The city streets turned into Hwy 36 as they left Farley behind them. The road was lined with green pastures, lazy cows, and budding trees. Spring was here. And it all felt good to her eyes and to her spirit. She needed this ride after this morning.

"There were perfumes today."

"Mom said she saw a package delivered. She asked me if you had gotten a lot of packages lately. I told her the truth. That there were roses on your doorstep, gifts at your door."

"Oh do you think that was wise? I mean—I know she's your mom, but will she repeat it? I just don't want to be the gossip of Farley."

"She understands that. She was the one to tell me to keep my mouth closed on the subject. That you didn't need it told all over town."

"I like your mom. She's very sensible."

"I never thought about it, but yeah, I guess she is.

Every morning she's outside working in her flowerbeds. She thinks she has to have flowers all year long."

"I just wish mom would take up a hobby. I worry about her. What is she going to do once I'm gone?"

"You make it sound like you won't ever come around after the wedding."

"That's not what I mean, but she doesn't even take care of her own cooking or laundry. Nothing. Do you know what she was doing when I got up this morning?" She didn't wait for a reply. "Cooking rolls. She had flour all over the kitchen. How can she forget how to cook?"

"Did the rolls turn out ok?"

"I don't know. I came back downstairs and she was gone. The kitchen is still a mess. I told her it was hers. I just hope she cleans it before..." She almost said before Harvey came. But she didn't want to think about Harvey. Not now. If she did she would feel guilty. She didn't want to feel guilty.

He turned off 36 and she knew where they were going. He looked at her and grinned as the car sped up the long mountain known as The Hill. There should be no one here in the middle of the day. He parked the car under the large oak not far from the waterfall that was the main attraction of the hill, that and the serenity. He took out a basket from the trunk, and a light blue blanket that lay next to the basket. He threw the blanket across his arm.

"I went to the deli and got us sandwiches, a roasted chicken, potato salad, and yeast rolls." He spread the blanket, then sat the basket on the blanket and began to remove the food. "Sit," he said, pointing to a place next to him.

He had plates, napkins, forks, and glasses. "I thought

about a bottle of wine, but I figured you would object so I bought a bottle of Coke."

"Yes," she said, a smile playing with her mouth, "Coke is better. I don't need the wine."

"Why? You don't trust yourself with a good looking man?"

"It has to be me. I was told I could trust the good looking man."

He poured her a drink. Tore off a piece of chicken and placed it on a plate, which he handed to her. "Oh, you can. I know him personally and he is a fine man. Very good looking, and very fine."

She laughed. It was so easy to laugh with him.

"Here," he dropped a spoon full of potatoes onto her plate. They landed with a loud thug.

"Give me that," she teased, "before you have food all over both of us."

He handed the bowl to her and she served his plate. "Baked beans? You didn't say you had baked beans," she said as she removed a lid from a bowl. "I love baked beans."

"Oh, yeah. We also have a German Chocolate cake for dessert. And here…" He dug into the basket and brought up a small metal can.

"What is that?"

"Salmons."

"Just what are you doing with a can of salmons?"

"Don't you remember? We always went fishing up here. Here, catch." He pitched the can to her. She laughed as she caught it. "And you don't have to worry about cleaning them." He grinned as he took the plate of food from her.

She bit into the warm yeast roll that had been rolled into a cloth to keep it warm. The chicken was tender, the beans spicy, and her heart happy.

"How did you know this was the best place for lunch?"

"Because we decided a long time ago that there was no place in Farley better than the Hill. It didn't matter if we were eating a jelly sandwich or fighting off aliens, the hill was the place to be."

"The waterfall is the same."

The waterfall was behind them in the distance. It fell over rocks, about three feet, ran about two feet and then fell again seven feet into the pond below then making its way down the hillside. It was a double fall.

"I leave Saturday."

"Saturday?"

"Yeah, if not tomorrow. I have to go back to my home office, then leave for Africa. I wish you were coming with me."

"David, don't."

"I'm not. Just thinking aloud. I think it would be good for you." She didn't answer. He rolled over on his stomach, gazing at the falls. "If we were ten, we would walk through the falls."

"It's a little cool for that."

"Never stopped you back then."

"Maybe not, but I think we have grown up just a little…at least one of us."

"Oh, I don't know, El, I think you've grown up a little bit too."

"Why you." She poked him in the ribs, he laughed and rolled over on his back. "Eat your chicken."

He sat up, ate his chicken, the whole time grinning at

her.

"Stop doing that."

"What am I doing?"

"You know exactly what you are doing."

"No, I don't." He kept grinning. Then she laughed. A deep laughter that she could not control. It consumed her and he laughed because he thought it was funny she couldn't stop. Then he pulled her over on him and told her very softly.

"Don't get married." She stiffened. He said it again. "Don't get married. Come away with me."

She pushed him away. "You're teasing me, aren't you?"

"No. Never. El. Don't get married until you give us a chance."

"I can't do this. Harvey's coming tonight. I knew I shouldn't have come with you. Every time I think I can trust myself to be alone with you, you cause me to…"

"To what? Think about us?"

"How many times do I have to say it? There is no us. There has never been an us. There never will be. You have your life; I have mine. Can you not see this, David. It's because Carol left you. You are just trying to hold onto the past because the past is safe. You know how it all turns out."

"And what are you holding onto, El. Are you in love with Harvey? Or is he just safe?"

Harvey safe? She had never thought about it like that. Two weeks ago she would have told him she was madly in love with Harvey. But that was before her heart beat fast for David. A feeling that she enjoyed yet was ashamed of. She didn't even blush when she thought about David. But she had a secret she never told him. Never could.

She looked into those bold blue eyes and without even blinking, the horrible thought went through her mind.

What would it be like to make love to him?

And what made it worse—this wasn't the first time she had thought such since he had returned to town. For a woman who refused to think about sex in the past, it sure did enter her mind a lot now.

She waited to blush. Oh, how she wished she would blush. But she didn't. That just made it worse. It was as if this horrible person had taken over her body, giving her all these evil thoughts.

She shook her head.

"No, David, I don't think it would be a good idea for us?"

"You didn't answer my question."

What was the question? She couldn't ask him the question. She would just give a safe 'no'.

"No."

"Alright then." He pulled her to her feet. "At least walk with me through the waterfall."

"That water is freezing."

"So?" He laughed as he pulled her toward the fall. He sat down on the edge, removed his shoes, rolling up his pants legs. He sat the shoes aside, put his feet into the water. "OHHHH."

"I told you!"

"I double-dog dare you."

"Huh-uh, David, huh-uh." But she laughed, peeled off her shoes and rolled up her pants legs. Together, hand in hand they ran through the falls at the lower lever. Five feet of water sprayed them as they ran behind the falls.

Water droplets fell from their hair as they emerged on the other side. Their feet were wet, their clothes damp from the spray. But they laughed as two ten year olds.

"You owe me until the day we die for this one," Mary Ellen laughed.

"This is just paying you back for daring me to climb Mr. Barnhart's oak tree. He threatened to shoot me with a bb gun if I didn't get out of that tree. Remember?" She laughed. "Come on." He grabbed her hand.

He pulled her along behind him as they traveled to the top of the bluff from where the waterfall fell. Here the sun shone warmly upon the rocks. He lay spread-eagled on a wide sand rock. She stared at him for a moment, then he held his hand up to her. She took his hand and lay down beside him. Then she turned.

She laid her head on his stomach, spread her arms. It was the same way they lay twenty-five years earlier. Kids on warm summer days after they had waded in the forbidden falls. Their clothes had to be dried before they went home or else their parents would have whipped them both.

Chapter Twenty Three

The sun set at five forty-nine. A slight cool breeze stirred. Mary Ellen rolled over on her side, pulled her knees toward her chest, tucking her hands under her cheek. She felt a little chilled. David grunted. Her eyes flew open.

"Oh, my gosh, David!"

"What—what?" He tried to move but Mary Ellen was still lying on him. Quickly she rolled over on her hands and knees. He leaned upward, resting on his elbow and arms.

"Get up, David, get up! Quickly!"

He quickly jumped up as Mary Ellen scrambled to her feet. She made a three hundred sixty degree turn. "Oh, David! Oh, David! Where's the sun!"

"Just settle down, El. It's ok. We know where we are. See, there, the car."

"I know that. I'm not some dim-wit! Don't you realize what this means?"

Not really, but he didn't think he should say that. Instead it was best to keep her calm. "Give me your hand, El, I'll get us down."

She was in front of him. It was clear she didn't need his help getting down. Then it hit him. Harvey! Harvey was coming for dinner. Harvey would be at her house any minute if not already there. She was saying something, but he couldn't tell what. He ran to catch up with her.

"I don't know what I'm going to tell him. He is going to be so mad. He will be right there on that porch when we pull back up in your drive. You're going to have to let me out down the street. I can't let him see me like this. I'm going to have to sneak into the house, change clothes and come down the back stairs."

He couldn't say a word she was talking so fast. Surely she would have to catch her breath, but the words just kept spilling out of her mouth. Finally he interrupted.

"Maybe he won't get mad, maybe he will understand."

She stopped so quickly, he bumped into her. "Have you lost your mind? You do not know this man! Have you even thought about what you just said? No, of course not. Spoken just like a man. What would you do if your girlfriend went off with another man and came home in wet clothes?"

She turned around, not waiting for his answer. Which was just as well. Their clothes weren't wet any longer. But he wasn't able to mention that. If he did, he would have to mention her beet-red face. He would let her worry about that when she got home. Make-up should take care of that for her. At least his face didn't burn. The advantage of a tan.

Within ten minutes they were home. He talked Mary Ellen into not getting out of his car. Instead they drove by her house. If Harvey's car was in the drive, they would not stop and he would take her around to the back alley. To their delight, more Mary Ellen's than his, Harvey's car was no where to be seen.

David pulled into the drive. Mary Ellen flew up the steps and disappeared into the house. Alice was sitting on her front porch when David pulled into their drive.

"Was that Mary Ellen I saw getting out of your car?"

"Yes, ma'am."

"She sure was in a hurry. Harvey must be coming over. I don't think you should be taking such chances. She is getting married in a few days."

"I know. Eight days, I believe."

"Yes, a week from Saturday."

"A week from Saturday I will be in Africa."

"Should be at that wedding."

"Why do you say that?"

"You two have been friends for so long. You were the brother she never had and she your sister. Wouldn't you agree?" Alice moved her rocker slowly. David opened the screen door. "Supper will be ready in a few minutes."

He eased through the door. He didn't agree with her about Mary Ellen, and he wasn't interested in supper. He saw Harvey's car pull into the drive next door. Wonder if El made it to her room without being seeing? If it weren't for the feeling that was eating away at him, today would have reminded him of their youth.

He went into his bedroom. The bag sat on the floor ready for his departure. Tomorrow he should leave. There was no point in saying good-bye to El. If he did, there would be the risk he might say something foolish again.

Why did he walk away from her when they entered Junior High? But he knew. Girls. If El were his best friend, the boys would have called him a sissy. The girls would have thought she was his girlfriend. There was too much to do in junior high. And he didn't need a sixth grade kid hanging onto him. The older he got, the younger she got. Or so it seemed.

He never would have thought he would have asked her to marry him. Maybe she was right. Maybe he was just messed up because of Carol.

He would leave tomorrow. Early.

Chapter Twenty Four

"Mary Ellen, Harvey's here." Gladys stood at the foot of the stairs, calling upward, her voice filling the house. "Mary Ellen." She saw her dash in like a mad woman, ran up the stairs two at a time. Right behind her was Harvey knocking on the door. This should be a very interesting dinner. So far all they were having were rolls. She had prepared the rolls when she returned from her little trip. She even got the kitchen cleaned up.

She got everything taking care of. Mary Ellen would be in for quiet a surprise next Saturday.

"I'm coming, Mother. Just a few minutes." Hastily she raked her fingers through her hair. The clothes would have to do and just hope he didn't notice she didn't have on fresh make-up. The make-up from this morning probably washed off at the falls.

She jerked open the door and rushed from her room, then stopped just outside the door. Thank goodness she beat Harvey home. She took a deep breath and walked slowly toward the stairs, her hand gliding over the banister as if she didn't have a care in the world.

"Harvey, darling, I'm so glad you're here," she cooed. She noticed the snug expression on her mother's face but chose to ignore it. She floated down the stairs, hand stroking the rail.

When she reached Harvey, she smiled boldly at him. He did not return her smile, but stared at her.

"Where were you today, Mary Ellen?"

So that's why her mother looked so smug. He called and she told him she was out. Ok. No big deal.

"I called and no one answered."

So he didn't talk to her mother. Why is she looking at her so peculiar?

"Mary Ellen?" Harvey demanded.

"I went out for awhile. No where in particular. Just went for a…" Her mind went blank. Why on earth doesn't her mother stop looking at her like that?

"Is there something wrong, mom?" she innocently asked.

"No. I was just wondering about your face?"

Mary Ellen's hand went to her face. "My face?"

"What did you do, Mary Ellen, lay out in the sun?" Harvey asked.

"My face?" She went to the mirror that hung near the coat tree. She gasped!

"Why is your face so burned?" Gladys asked.

Her hand went to her face as if she could hide it. Then with a nervous laugh she turned to face them. "This is so silly. It was such a foolish thing to do. I fell asleep in the sun. I just didn't think about it being that hot or that I would fall asleep." She knew her face felt hot, but she thought it was because she had been in a rush. Not because it looked like a beet.

"Mary Ellen, you're a grown woman! There's no sense in acting like a kid, burning your face up!" scolded

Harvey. "I can see right now, you and I are going to have to have a long talk. I will not have my wife acting like this." Then he took a deep breath, blew it out as if he were a prize bull, threw his head back, shoulders straight "And it will make you appear old."

Gladys stood against the side of the stair rail, listening—a smile touching her lips. Appear old. Ha! She would still be years younger than him! So the old boy is laying down the law. Can you not see what kind of life you will have with this man, Mary Ellen! Come on—get mad—tell him to buzz off.

But instead Mary Ellen dropped her head. "I'm sorry, Harvey. It won't happen again."

Just like that? She's sorry. For what? What did she do? Fall asleep in the sun. Good grief! Can this child of mine not have any kind of backbone, Gladys thought. Never would Norbert have talked to her like this—nor would she have allowed him to do so. Why is she so mealy-mouth?

Gladys straightened up from the rail. "And I guess while you were lying around in the sun you didn't have time to fix any dinner, did you?" See if that will goad her just a little.

Dinner? Oh no. Dinner. Why couldn't her mother for once cook dinner? Would it have killed her!

"Well...well...I...I just forget all about dinner. I'll...I...it won't take but just a few minutes. I'll have a nice dinner for you, Harvey." She took his hat, perched it on the coat tree. "You just have a seat and watch TV or read your evening paper. Won't be but just a minute." She rushed for the kitchen.

And almost made it before her mother spoke.

"When is David leaving?"

Harvey stopped. He had almost made it to the big chair in the living room, but he stopped right where he was. He turned. Cold eyes met Gladys' dancing mischievous ones.

"Is he that fellow who drives the red sport car?"

"Oh yes, that's him," Gladys informed. "Nice young man. He and Mary Ellen were always such good friends." She turned back to Mary Ellen who froze in her steps, her back to Harvey and her mother. She didn't move. She couldn't move. She was waiting for the bomb to drop. And it would drop. She knew her mother. "Did he say when he was leaving? Is he going to go before the wedding?"

Questions. All those questions. She knew what she was doing. Why was she doing this? Why was she so set against Harvey? Her mother knew Harvey didn't kill his wife. Who cares where he came from? Or why he was here. He was going to be her husband in eight days.

She felt weak.

Eight days she would walk down the aisle to this man her mother was accusing of murder. This man whom her mother enjoyed tormenting. What kind of married life would she have with a mother and husband who despised one another? And a husband who would dominate her? Oh David why did you come back?

"No, mother," she said without turning. "Soon. That's all I know."

"Oh, I thought perhaps he mentioned it when he came over this morning."

"What was he doing here this morning?" Harvey asked.

"He just ran by for a few minutes," Mary Ellen

explained.

"Ran? Ha! I'll say! The way he took those stairs he was running alright," laughed Gladys.

"Stairs? He was upstairs with you."

"Well—yes—I was upstairs, so he came up."

Hum. He had never been upstairs with her. He was marrying her and never had he been in her bedroom. Come to think of it—he had never been alone with her in the house. Mouth was always here.

"Mary Ellen," he said sternly, "look at me." She turned slowly. "Tell me what that man was doing here this morning—in your bedroom?"

"It wasn't like that, Harvey. Tell him, mother." Pleading eyes met her mother's.

"Well, no, of course not. David's not that kind of man."

"Mother!" Her voice hit a new high note.

"Nor is Mary Ellen. I mean…now Harvey," Gladys patronized, " you don't have anything to worry about. He wasn't here that long. Ran right up those stairs and I'll say within five minutes he came right back down them. Of course, he was in a much better mood when he came back down them, though." She turned to her daughter. "Mary Ellen, you never told me why he came by."

"I didn't think I needed to, Mother. I didn't realize I was to report everything to you."

"No, dear, of course not."

"But you do to me," retorted Harvey. "And I'm still waiting."

Mary Ellen stared at him. Her face hurt from the sunburn. Her body was tired and dirty, her hair limp. And her heart was heavy from all the lies. Her shoulder slumped from the weight of everything.

"Ok," she said. "Ok. Ok, if you want to know everything. Here it is. David came over here this morning because I accused him of sending the roses. Then when I tried to apologize, he hung up the phone...'

"I thought you said he came by, not on the phone..."

"Shut up, Harvey. If you want to hear this, then just shut up till I am finished. Then say what you will.

"He stormed over here, demanding I apologize, which I did. Then he kissed me..."

"He what?" Harvey shouted.

"Let her finish, Harvey, let her finish," Gladys encouraged. Oh, this was getting good. He kissed her!

"Then he told me to meet him at his house and we would go to lunch. I thought we were going somewhere in town, but we went up on the Hill..."

"What's the hill?" Harvey wanted to know, but Mary Ellen kept talking without answering him.

"...and he had brought a picnic lunch. We walked under the waterfall—got wet—and we lay in the sun to dry. We fell asleep. It was sundown when we woke up and that why my face is burned and what I have been doing all day, and that's why there's no dinner."

She turned to face her mother. "Satisfied?"

Gladys smiled. "Whatever makes you happy, dear, makes me happy," she answered sweetly.

"Well, I'm not happy," Harvey roared. "Just who do you think you are going around kissing other men, going on a picnic, and laying around in the sun?"

"He kissed her—Harvey, that's not the same."

"Stay out of this, Gladys. Don't get me started on you."

"Started on me!" Gladys bellowed, her hands on her hips. "Started on me, will you."

"Mother, please..."

Gladys looked at Mary Ellen. The expression on her face cooled Gladys' tongue. It was sadness she saw on Mary Ellen's face. The joy of her approaching wedding, the bliss of becoming Mrs. Harvey Broyhill had been lost in all the turmoil of the last few days.

Gladys walked out on the porch, leaving Harvey and Mary Ellen standing in the front hallway. She sat down in the wicker swing. She could hear them talking, wishing Mary Ellen would stand her ground, knowing she would not.

"It meant nothing, Harvey. He's just upset about his divorce. We were kids together. Grew up right here. Don't you think if we were going to get together, we would have fifteen years ago. Can't you see that?"

"I see this man who has come into town, upset you, and all these gifts and roses started at the same time. How do you know it isn't him? And how can I know you are really telling me the truth? If you lie to me once, will you not lie to me again if given the opportunity?"

"Harvey, how can you say that?" Hurt filled her voice.

"It's true. Lies breed lies."

Mary Ellen turned away. She didn't want him to see her wipe the tears from her eyes. Maybe he was right. She didn't tell him everything. She didn't tell him about the foolish question David asked her.

Harvey caught her shoulders. He squeezed them. Too tightly. But she didn't cry out. She didn't want him to know the pain she felt. She stood there. Strong. Back straight. And waited for his next words. Was the wedding off? Did she want him to say that?

"We won't have any more lies, will we, Mary Ellen?" She shook her head. "You will be a respectful wife. I will have no other. Do you understand that?" This time she nodded her head. "Stay away from that man." Again she nodded. He turned her to face him.

"Where's the rose and today's gift?"

"I threw the rose away. Mother took the perfumes. I don't know what she did with them."

Gladys heard them, but she made no move to tell them where the perfumes were.

Chapter Twenty Five

Dinner was ready by seven. Gladys was quiet proud of Mary Ellen. She was surprised she was able to prepare the meal after the spat with Harvey. But the meal was good. She had taken a canned ham, sliced it, placed it in a swallow dish with brown sugar and pineapples. She then baked it in the microwave for a minute.

She also baked Van Camp's Pork & Bean with brown sugar, a toss of mustard and onions, and ketchup. She placed those in the microwave too. It was as if she opened every can in the house. There was corn, green beans, boiled potatoes, beets, and Gladys didn't know where this came from, but a small can of salmons.

"Been a long time since I've eaten salmons," Harvey said. He pushed the food into his mouth. A large slice of ham lay on his plate. "You're a good cook, Mary Ellen. Fine cook."

And she will make you a good cook, thought Gladys. Always the submissive, agreeable little wife. Deep in thought, she stirred her beans. "How many times have you been married, Harvey?"

"I beg your pardon?"

"Mildred? Was that your only wife?"

"Yes, of course. Why would you ask such a question?"

"I just wondered. I—we don't know a lot about you."

"Seems kinda late in the game to be asking questions, isn't it Mrs. Forsman? After all, Mary Ellen knows all she needs to know about me or she would have never agreed to be my wife."

"Is that true, Mary Ellen? Do you know all you need to know about Harvey?"

"Mother, please." It had been such a long day and she didn't want to go through this.

"But it is a good question. It's only a little over a week until it will be too late for questions. You will be on your honeymoon…"

"Mother!" she laid her fork down calmly. No one— not her mother—not Harvey—not even herself was going to upset her again tonight. "I have no questions for Harvey. I trust Harvey. We have no secrets."

But that was a lie too. She did not tell him that David asked her to marry him. But that didn't matter. He didn't mean it. David was going away. She would never see him again. She didn't love David. She loved Harvey. She needed Harvey's steady hand. A home. Babies. No— there would never be any babies. No babies not now…not ever…

"As it should be." Harvey smiled at his bride to be.

"And what about you, Harvey, do you have any secrets you didn't tell Mary Ellen?" Gladys prodded.

"Mother, what are you trying to do?"

"No, Mary Ellen, it's ok. It's obvious what she is attempting. But I can assure you, I don't mind your questions, Mrs. Forsman. There are no secrets. None."

"Then tell me why you came here?"

"I already have, but if it appeases you, I will tell you

again. I—Mildred and I moved here because I needed a job. There was a job here at this paper. Quiet simple. Just a job move. Of course we never dreamed she would become ill. If we had known, we would have stayed near the children. Gloria would not have had to move here. Her brothers are so far away."

"And that's in Denver?"

"Denver? Oh, no…not Denver. Denton. Denton, Texas. North West of Dallas."

"But I thought you said Denver."

"I know. But I never said Denver. You did."

"Why did you lead me to believe it was Denver?" Gladys asked. Hot anger boiled beneath the surface, but her voice was steady. She did not want him to be able to gloat over her mistake.

"I didn't want to insult you by correcting you. I know with age some times you can not hear well…"

"I can hear quiet well, thank you for your concern."

"I guess now I know why your police officer friend came by the office today. Asking a few questions. I wondered why he thought I was from Denver." He smiled. "Then I remembered. You thought it was Denver."

But it wasn't a pleasant smile. It reminded Gladys of a rat who snatched the cheese from the trap without being caught, and now was enjoying his prize.

"Mother, you didn't send Nathan to question Harvey, did you?"

"Of course not!" Gladys snapped. And Mr. Nathan would be hearing from her! Telling her to keep her mouth shut and he goes to the wolf. What's got into the boy!

"Yes, he had some very interesting questions. All kinds of questions about Mildred. How long was she sick?

Was she under a doctor's care while we lived in Denton? It was amazing how interested he was."

"Mother!"

"I did not tell that man to go see Harvey." Boldly she looked into his eyes. "But I would love to hear the answers."

Harvey laughed. A loud deep laugh. "Oh Mrs. Forsman, you just won't do." He turned to Mary Ellen. "Why don't you let your mother clear the table tonight and we'll go for a nice walk?" He glanced at Gladys. "You wouldn't mind doing that for two love- birds would you, Mrs. Forsman. I'm sure you remember how it was with you and your future husband when you were young. Such a nice night." He stood, pulled back Mary Ellen's chair. "We appreciate this so much."

He took Mary Ellen's hand and led her from the room and out the front door. Gladys did not respond. She just sat there. Thinking. She had to do something. She just wasn't for sure what. One thing she knew she wasn't going to do was clear Harvey's plate.

She took her plate and Mary Ellen's into the kitchen. She washed the two plates, put the leftovers in the refrigerator and went to the living room.

She couldn't wait to get hold of that Nathan. If she knew where he lived, she would go to his house and demand just what did he think he was doing? But, he would be here later tonight. She'd get him then. He was supposed to be here at nine. Harvey should be gone by then. That had been her plan, have Harvey out of the way so he wouldn't be suspicious.

Ha! Nathan did exactly what he told her not to do. Mention anything to Harvey. And now Harvey lets her know that her officer had dropped by to see him—with a lot of questions. Denton. Denton, Texas? She'd never heard of Denton. Could he be lying about that too?

She wished Nathan would call. Should have written down the number when she had the chance. The station wouldn't give her his number even if they didn't know who she was, and it sure wouldn't help to tell them she knew him.

She sat in the big chair, flipped on the TV. She flipped the channels. There was supposed to be an old rerun of *Perry Mason*. Where was it? She flipped. Click. Click. Then she stopped. It was a five minutes recap of the evening news and there stood Nathan.

He was saying something about a body out on Hwy 36. A woman found dead in her yard.

Guess he did have something to do beside chase a rose dropper.

The next morning at six o'clock Mary Ellen got out of bed and went into the bathroom. She turned on the shower. She should have taken the bath last night, but Harvey stayed so late, she was just too tired to bother. She thought he would never leave. Almost as if he was making sure it was too late for any other visitors.

They went for a long walk down the sidewalk. Then they watched a movie on TV. Gladys went to bed early. Saying something about a murder out on Hwy 36. Harvey asked her if this one was real. She didn't respond, but went upstairs. Later when she came to bed, Mary Ellen heard snoring coming from Gladys' bedroom. She decided her mother wasn't too upset over Harvey's remarks.

The water was refreshing, washing away yesterday's grim and troubled emotions. She loved Harvey. She loved him two weeks ago and she loved him this morning.

She had to love him. She had a wedding dress hanging in the closet; a diamond on her finger; invitations mailed.

Oh, my gosh! she gasped. She had forgotten about the invitations. They should have been mailed out over a week ago. The day of the first rose should have been the day the invitations were mailed. She was perturbed over roses and forgot the invitations. A wedding with no guests. And Harvey's ring. She didn't go pick it up either.

What was the matter with her? As if she didn't know. She slammed the wall with her wet palm!

Quickly she finished her shower and dressed. She took the stairs two at a time. Gladys was coming through the front door.

"You sure are in a good mood. Stepping high."

"Good mood has nothing to do with it. Would you believe I forgot to mail the invitations?" She didn't give Gladys time to answer but went to the roll top desk in the living room. She removed the two hundred cream colored envelopes.

Gladys stood in the wide archway that led from the front foyer into the living room. "I guess you won't have to bother sending David one."

Mary Ellen turned. Puzzlement covered her face. "What do you mean? I know he's leaving."

"This morning?"

"This morning? No."

"Just saw him throwing bags in that little red car. He got in. Left."

Mary Ellen stood holding the invitations. She couldn't believe it. He didn't even bother to say good-by. Why didn't he say good-by?

She moved toward the door.

"Too late to catch him."

"That's not what I had in mind. I've got to get these to the post office."

She reached the door before Gladys asked, "You want this?" She held the yellow rose in her hand. The green tissue paper held snug with a white ribbon.

"No. Throw it in the trash. I don't care who it is. He will not ruin my wedding or my future."

"No, I think you're doing a fine job all by yourself."

She whirled. Fire flashed from her eyes. "Ok, that does it. I have put up with your remarks for the last ten years. Just because your world ended when daddy passed doesn't mean mine did. This is my time. Do you hear me—my time. I won't let you or anyone take it from me. If you have something against Harvey, why didn't you say so that first night? Why now? What has he done to turn you against him?"

"Nothing. Not a thing. And you know, that makes this statement even more important. I just got to know him. The more I knew him, the less I liked him. More questions kept popping into my head. Questions that you would never ask. But maybe you should."

"And you should be thinking about in one week you will be left all alone in this big old house. What are you going to do then?"

"Oh, that's where you're wrong."

"And what's that suppose to mean?"

"Oh, you'll see—you'll see."

Mary Ellen slammed the door. Gladys threw the rose in the garbage.

Chapter Twenty Six

The package was lying on the swing when Gladys came home. Around ten she had gone on an important errand. Something she had been working on for the last three days. Today she finalized all the details. Mary Ellen would be in for a big surprise next Saturday.

Alice Petrie was in her flowerbed pulling weeds when Gladys started up the walk. Alice saw Gladys through the fence. She quickly stood.

"Gladys, I laid the package in the swing. I noticed no one came to the door. Someone sure is sending wedding gifts." She propped her arm up on the fence. "Have they decided where they are going to live?"

"What? Who?"

"Mary Ellen and her beau."

Beau! She hadn't heard that word in years. Just goes to show how old and out of touch Alice Petrie is!

"Here in Farley. Harvey has a house here."

"So they aren't going to move in with you? Well, I know you will miss her. Mary Ellen is such a sweet friendly girl. Harvey is getting a fine young woman."

Gladys moved on up the walk. Alice was saying something else, but Gladys didn't hear her. She didn't want to talk to Alice Petrie. They had been neighbors for thirty years. And she had never wanted to chat with Alice Petrie over the fence. Alice Petrie was not her friend, nor her neighbor. She just happened to be the person who lived next door to her house. She just happened to be the mother of her daughter's childhood playmate. That same child who kissed her daughter.

She turned around. She didn't go to the fence, but she spoke loud enough for Alice to hear her and old man Peters if he had been sitting on his front porch across the street.

"How come your son left town so fast? And another thing—that divorce of his—was he running around on his wife? And what was he doing over here kissing my daughter?"

Alice Petrie's mouth dropped open.

"Well, are you going to answer me or just stand there goggling?"

"I'll have you know when my son leaves town is none of your business and further more, his divorce isn't elocution to be discussed on street corners. But if you must know, no, he was not running around on his wife," she replied placidly, yet sternly.

"I don't know why he kissed Mary Ellen. When did this happen? Maybe it was a good-bye kiss. He does have a job to go back to! There is more to life than Farley." She could feel her temper rising. How that sweet girl could have this brute for a mother just proves God has a sense of humor. That was the only explanation for it!

"Well—yeah—" Gladys was surprised at her comeback. She couldn't think of anything to say. In fact, she didn't even know why she had asked the question in the first place. She turned and started up the front steps. Then it hit her!

Why didn't Mary Ellen fall in love with David when they were kids? David should have been her son-in-law. Not Harvey.

She moaned softly as she picked up the package and put her key into the brass lock.

Once inside she hung her purse on the coat tree. Her gray sweater was hung on top of the purse. She still held the package in her hand. It was wrapped just like all the others. It was about the size of a shirt box.

She pulled off the brown paper, letting it fall to the floor. Inside was a purple box. She lifted the lid revealing pink tissue paper laying in soft folds. She touched the paper delicately, lifting it and peering underneath.

Gladys dropped the box as she pulled out the garment. The label read, Laura Ashley poet shirt... fine intimate apparel. It was soft and pink, ruffled collar and cuffs with a thin tie string at the neck.

No card.

Why would a man buy such pretty gifts and just leave them. How was this supposed to woo her daughter to him? All it was doing was pulling Mary Ellen and Harvey into arguments—which was bad in itself. Anything to keep the happy couple at each other's throats.

Maybe that was the game plan. It wasn't really working...but maybe...

Now just who did she and Mary Ellen know that would have been smitten by the beauty of her fair daughter, yet to timid to admit his love? It had to be someone from church—or the grocery store—perhaps the mall. Where else did Mary Ellen go?

No where that she knew of.

She draped the pink poet shirt over the big chair. She still wanted to talk to Nathan. When she was out, she went by the police station, but they told her he was out of the office. Nathan was busy with his murder case.

She wondered who killed the woman? A lover— husband? Most murders are committed by people the victim knows—or at least according to Perry Mason.

She wondered if Nathan would just walk into the husband's office and asked him if he killed his wife? She was still angry at him for talking to Harvey. He blew her whole cover.

She hadn't really thought of it as a cover before, but just how was she supposed to find out anything if he tells Harvey she's suspicious of him?

She picked up the phone. She dialed, then waited.

"Yes, this is Gladys Forsman. I just wanted to know if I may speak with Officer Nathan Oneal?"

"Just a moment please."

So he was back. Good. He had some explaining to do.

"Oneal here."

"Nathan, Gladys. Just why on earth did you go to Harvey and ask him all those questions?"

"Oh, hi, Gladys. How's things going? Mary Ellen still getting roses?"

"Yes, Mary Ellen is still getting roses and gifts! You didn't answer my question."

"I checked around. Everything kept coming to a dead end. I just decided the best thing to do was go talk to the guy. Seemed surprised I was asking him about his dead wife. But that was no surprise for me. Anyway, he's from Denton, Texas—not Denver, Colorado. That explained why I couldn't find anything on him.

"Anyway, I checked him out and he's what he says. Has a good name in the community. Well respected family. Her doctor was surprised she was dead though. But he said that was the way of ovarian cancer. Sneaks up on a person."

"And you believe that's what happened. Ovarian cancer sneaked into her life and not Harvey?"

"That's how it all looks, Gladys. Maybe you feel this way because the wedding is so close. Perhaps it would be best if you just accepted him."

"And the roses—just accept that too?"

"I didn't say that. The only way to catch this guy is to just wait up on him. He's coming every night. It's not like you don't know where he's going to be. Some time after you have gone to bed, he shows. It shouldn't be that hard to catch him."

"But you said…"

"I said, don't approach him."

"Well, I didn't know if that was still your advice or not after finding out about your little talk with Harvey."

"Harvey is the one who should be sitting up with Mary Ellen to catch this character." He paused. "I'd help, but since this murder happened—there's just no way. Do you want me to send Tony over? Just in case the guy shows."

She almost felt as if she was a woman being brushed off by her lover. The excuses were plentiful, the mood changed from one of casual concern to dismissal. It was no big deal—he had bigger cases to solve—more impressive criminals to catch.

"No," she said, "don't bother."

She hung up the phone. A heavy sigh passed her lips. No longer did she fear the person who sneaked onto her porch in the middle of the night to leave a yellow rose for her daughter. If he had been able to break the engagement, she might have invited him in for tea...or better still, hugged his neck.

But the wedding was still on. The dropper was no closer to being caught, nor was the engagement broken. In one week, Mary Ellen would be married. At least she did feel a little better knowing that Harvey didn't murder his wife—or so says the law of Farley.

"Mother!" Mary Ellen burst through the front door. "I know who the dropper is!"

Gladys jumped up out of the big chair and rushed to Mary Ellen. "Who?" she cried.

"Joey Henson!"

"Joey Henson! That little ole pip-squeak who plays the harp at church? I don't believe that! Why on earth do you think it's him? I doubt if his mother would even let him out of the house at night. How old is that boy anyway?"

"I don't know. Old enough to buy roses and yes, he is old enough to be out at night. I ran into him at the post office. When he saw what I had in my hand he said—now get this—'I would have thought you already had those mailed out. Not too much excitement at your house to make you forget, is it?'"

"Go on."

"That's it."

"That's it? And you think he is sending you the roses because of that," she scoffed.

"How does he know about the chaos that we have been having here? Tell me that? And you should have seen that smirk on his face when he saw me with those invitations."

She paced the floor as her imagination washed over her as freely as the waters from the waterfall flowing down the hill. "He's not in love—he's bored. Yeah, that's it. And he knew about the wedding—knew this would cause all kinds of questions, problems. He did it all just for aggravation!"

"Mary Ellen," she said placidly, "do you really believe this—this—I don't even know what to call him—what? Kid—"

"He's not a kid, Mother, that much I know. He's at least—I don't know—but he's out of school—has a job—" She whirled around, her face gleaming with excitement. "And guess what kind of job he has, mother, guess."

"Well—I don't know—let me think..." She couldn't think. Had she ever even heard anyone say what the young, slim, tattered red-hair boy did—other than play the harp for the church choir?

"Flowers, mother, he works with flowers."

"Oh..."

"He works at Marcia's Florist. That's perfect. It's him. I just know it is."

"Why, Mary Ellen? Why would this boy want to ruin your wedding? He would have to be some kind of nut!"

"Don't you see it! No one would ever think this mild mannered young man would be capable of doing this. He's the last person anyone would suspect."

"And I still don't see it."

"Well, I do. And tonight I will prove it. I will be right here in this hallway, waiting for him to lay that rose on the doorstep. Then you'll see..."

"Um," Gladys replied. She walked to the front door, lifting the lace curtain. She saw no one, but she didn't expect to. "David left."

Mary Ellen didn't respond.

"Alice said he had a job to get back to."

Still no response.

"Said his wife was running around on him. Didn't he tell you that?"

"We discussed his divorce. A little."

"Too bad he didn't come home more often. I think you and he would have made a nice couple."

"Oh, mother, please. Is that what's been bothering you these last few days. Thinking something was between David and me?"

"No." She let the curtain drop. She turned slowly around. "I just thought maybe you thought there was."

"What—what do you mean?"

"The way you were always ready to run off with him. Picnics—longs drives. Just thought maybe…"

She didn't look at her mother. She couldn't. If she did, Gladys might see what was truly in her soul through her eyes. She wouldn't risk that. David was gone. David wasn't coming back. It had been a fun few days. But now she had to come back to reality. And reality was she had promised herself to Harvey. In seven days she would be married, and someday David would drive back into town with a new bride on his arm.

And the last few days would fade into a memory that would rise only slightly as the years passed. Warm summer days would stir the memory and bring back in focus the waterfall and his words of love that he should have spoken long ago. Long before she promised herself to someone else and long before he took a wife that didn't really want him.

"No, mother, David and I are only friends. Friends

who will always have the past but no future."

"Oh," Gladys said softly as she walked out onto the porch. She felt sad.

Chapter Twenty Seven

Gladys went down the wide porch steps.

Alice was still working in her flowerbeds. How a body could spend all day long in a flowerbed just didn't make any sense to her. She bet Alice had never watched the first soap. She didn't know what good stories she was missing. Probably never watched *Perry Mason* re-runs either.

Gladys decided to go behind the house to sit in the backyard swing. It would be nice and peaceful. She wouldn't have to contend with Alice Petrie.

She figured the reason Alice worked so much in her yard was because it allowed her to see everything on the street—be able to know just what everyone was doing. Nosey old bitty. That was probably why she sat in the park feeding birds too. People think she was feeling sorry for the birds but in truth she was just watching people.

She walked along side the house, pushing back a limb from the willow tree that Norbert planted fifteen years ago. Made a nice tree. But she hated the little branches that it was always dropping even though, Mary Ellen kept them picked up.

"Gladys—Gladys. Gladys! Hold on a minute."

Alice Petrie had seen her. Gladys heard her the first time she called, but she didn't want to hear her. Oh, why—oh, why didn't she go out the back door!

She stopped. Slowly she turned to face her adversary. Alice was standing at the white picket fence, bonnet hovering over her eyes, small garden shovel in her gloved hand.

"Yes?"

"Did Mary Ellen like the gift?"

"Gift?"

"The one that came this morning I laid in the swing."

Oh yeah—the gift. She wondered if Mary Ellen would notice the nightshirt on the chair—or rather the poet shirt as the little tag stated.

"I don't know. We were discussing something else when she returned."

Alice smiled warmly. "Well, I'm sure she will. All wedding gifts are such a blessing. I know when my wedding was drawing near, I was so excited I couldn't hardly sleep nor eat. Oh, the bliss of an approaching wedding. Almost as wonderful as expecting a new baby." She smiled warmly again.

Gladys just stared at her. She could not imagine Alice Petrie as a young girl awaiting her wedding day...all bright and excited. She couldn't imagine Alice Petrie as a young woman even though she wasn't very old when they moved next door. Somewhere over the years all she could see was Alice Petrie—old...gray...nosey...dried up little old woman sitting on the park bench or bent over in her flowerbeds. A young excited girl in love awaiting her wedding day? No, she just couldn't picture that about Alice Petrie.

"...and you know you will cry at the wedding," she was saying when Gladys turned her back to her. "I cried so many tears at David's wedding. I just couldn't help it. My young man getting married."

Gladys whirled around. "You cry when he got divorced?" Gladys' words were direct. She was angry at David. She didn't realize that until just now. Angry that he left town. Angry that he didn't sweep Mary Ellen off her feet. Angry that he had given her, Gladys, hope that there would be a romance between the two. That's what it was. Hope. When she saw him kiss Mary Ellen, she felt hope that he would win Mary Ellen away from Harvey. But what did he do? Sneaked out of town without even a flip of his hat!

"I said, yes, Gladys. Did you hear me?" Alice replied dolorously.

"What?"

"I said yes, I cried when my David got a divorce. It is very painful when your child hurts."

Then she brightened. "How's Mary Ellen doing? She is such a sweet child. If I had had a daughter, I would have wanted her to be like your Mary Ellen."

Now how was she supposed to mouth off to that? That was the nicest thing she had ever heard Alice Petrie say. She always thought Alice would have figured her child would have been superior to Mary Ellen—not that he/she was of course.

"I guess you're excited about getting a new son-in-law?"

"Well…yeah…I mean…"

She felt guilty. She didn't know why. It wasn't her fault she had to lie. It was Alice's fault—asking all these nosey questions. What's she supposed to say? No, I don't want this man in my family—not as a son-in-law or anything else. I think he killed his wife so why would I want him marrying my daughter? I don't like him so…

She took a step closer to Alice Petrie. Alice was her Sunday School teacher. Had been for years. Did she ever tell a lie? Maybe I should stand a little closer to Alice just in case God thought about striking me with a bolt of lightning for lying.

But that was a foolish thought. A foolish thought for an old tired woman. Weary to the bone. She just couldn't do it again. Not again. No more lies.

"Alice…" She bit down hard on her lower lip. "I've got to ask you something."

"Yes?"

"When the delivery boy gave you that package, did he say anything—anything?"

"Well, no. I was just to make sure you got the package. Why was there something he was supposed to tell me?"

"No, I guess not."

Gladys turned away, then she looked back over her shoulder at the frail little woman standing there, peering out from under her bonnet, a smile on her face. The hand of God covering her heart and mind, Gladys decided, giving Alice that evasive peace that escaped her. She was tired. She needed rest more then the back yard swing could give. And she didn't want Mary Ellen to marry Harvey.

"Alice, just how well did you know Mildred Broyhill?"

"Well, I guess about as much as anyone in town. She was a quiet woman, very nice. I know she loved flowers. We would talk about flowers as we waited for class to begin. She seemed to be a very gracious woman. Why?"

"I just wondered. Never did really know her. You know how it is when a new person comes into the church…don't get to know everyone of them."

She was in your class, Alice thought, but she didn't say the words aloud. No sense in arguing with Gladys over that. Gladys had a quick tongue—always knew the 'come-back' remarks to make.

"Is there something troubling you, Gladys?"

She wanted someone to talk to, but deep in her heart she didn't trust Alice. She didn't want this spread all over town. She couldn't take the chance. Yet, Tony knew. Did he tell his dad?

"Have you seen anyone putting flowers on my porch?" she blurted.

Alice just stared at her momentarily. Then she smiled. "Why, Gladys, is someone giving you flowers?"

"No, you old bat! They're for Mary Ellen. Yellow roses." The words rushed from her before she could stop them. She didn't mean to call Alice an old bat. She always called her an old bat—just not aloud. Nor did she mean to speak of the roses—not this way.

Astonished, Alice gasped, "Well! You don't have to be so rude.'

"Look, I'm sorry." Gladys bit the words as if they were cold chucks of ice.

"For which part?" Alice responded just as cold. "The remark about my idiosyncrasy or for finally telling me about the rose?"

"You know?"

"Of course. My David told me about it. Said Mary Ellen didn't know who's sending them. Thought it was Harvey at first. Have you any ideas?"

"No. I wish I did. I don't understand why. It makes no sense."

"Perhaps the roses are to get Mary Ellen not to marry Harvey."

"If he wants to stop this marriage, he had better do something besides roses. Would you believe Mary Ellen thinks it's that young kid at church who plays the harp? I just can't see that. But after tonight, we'll know."

Alice appeared to be in deep thought before she responded. "You said they were yellow? How odd. One day while Mildred and I were discussing flowers, she said yellow roses were her favorite."

"Well, they're not Mary Ellen's!"

"What do you mean about after tonight you will know for sure who it is?"

"Mary Ellen said she was going to sit up all night and wait, that's what I mean."

"I see. Well, don't tell her what I said about Mildred liking yellow roses. I wouldn't want to make her feel uneasy—as if—well…"

"What, woman, speak up!"

"Just some people would feel a little strange to receive flowers that were the dead wife's favorite. Would hate for her to have second thoughts over such. Any chance Mary Ellen might call off the wedding?"

"Huh! She needs second thoughts. If I…" Then she stopped. She reminded herself just whom she was talking to. This was the nosiest woman in town and here she stood—Gladys Forsman—telling her every thought and event that had been happening for the last two weeks. She turned around without another word.

"Gladys, where are you going?" Gladys, true to her nature, refused to answer as she made her way to the back yard swing.

Chapter Twenty Eight

Dawn threw a gray light over Farley. Dawn revealed an empty porch at Mary Ellen's house. For the first time in over a week, there was no yellow rose on her doorstep.

Mary Ellen stood, stretched. It had been a long night as she waited. She had waited alone. Harvey said he had to get up to go to work. Gladys refused. Said it was Harvey's place to keep her protected on such matters. But she knew her mother did not go to bed. She could hear the floor overhead squeak as she moved about in her bedroom. Her mother couldn't rest either as they waited.

But no one came.

She walked slowly up the stairs. The room was dull gray as a new day sneaked into the house. She closed her bedroom door, closing out the world for a few hours as she lay down in her bed. Her eyes felt so heavy as sleep quickly swept over her tired body, but at eight-forty-five, she was abruptly awaken.

"Mary Ellen! Mary Ellen!" Gladys stood over her daughter's bed, shouting.

Mary Ellen jumped. Slowly she sat up. "What's wrong?"

"Look!" Gladys shoved the green tissue paper under Mary Ellen's nose. "I found it when I went out to get the morning paper. Laying there just like all the others. Did you see anyone last night?"

She pushed the flower away. "No." She ran her hands across her face. Then she threw back the sheet and got out of bed. "Get that thing away from me." Bewildered eyes stared into Gladys'. "Promise me, you have nothing to do with this."

"How can you say such?"

"I know you don't want this wedding. Everything points to you. You aren't afraid to eat the candy. You want the pin—I sit up all night waiting—and nothing. Now here you stand—telling me he came while I slept. What am I suppose to believe?"

"That I'm your mother and I would never do anything to hurt you—never."

"But who is doing this then?"

"I thought you said it was that kid at church."

"It has to be him."

Mary Ellen dashed to her closet. Removing a pair of jeans and a shirt, she quickly dressed. She pulled white socks from the dresser and picked up her tennis shoes from under the bed where she had left them the night before.

"Where are you going?"

"To see this guy. I know where he works. I'm going to have it out with him."

"I don't think you should do that, Mary Ellen. I just don't believe he's the guy."

"I do. And I'm going…"

The ringing phone interrupted her.

There was a phone in the hallway, and one in her mother's bedroom. But there had never been a phone in Mary Ellen's bedroom. Something else she just never had any use for.

The phone kept ringing.

"Aren't you going to answer it," she demanded.

"Well—I guess I can. It's probably Harvey. I don't know why you don't answer it. 'Course I don't understand why he isn't here with you when you sit waiting for who knows who…"

She went out into the hallway. "Hello," she roared into the mouthpiece. If Harvey wants to check on everything, let him come at midnight to keep Mary Ellen company.

"May I speak to Mary Ellen, please." It was Harvey.

"No. She's busy."

"What is she doing?"

"I can't tell you that either." Might as well needle him.

"Mrs. Forsman, I demand you put Mary Ellen on the phone this instant." Once they were married Gladys Forsman would no longer be a problem in his life. A loud buzzing sound filled his ear. His future mother-in-law had just hung up on him.

Mary Ellen tied her shoes, and without asking who was on the phone, ran down the stairs. Gladys heard the front door slam.

She was making a big mistake. She knew she was, but there was no way she could convince Mary Ellen. 'Bought wits best wits yet' her mother always told her.

Mary Ellen shoved open the door to the small florist. The shop was on the square in the middle of the street on the North side. The fragrance of flowers hit Mary Ellen nostrils as she entered. Marcia Williams glanced up as the little bell over the door jangled.

"Mary Ellen, how nice to see you. Are you here to

make sure I have those orders right?" she smiled. "Just a few more days!"

"No, I'm here to see Joey. Is he working today?"

"Yeah, but he won't be back until around twelve. He's delivering flowers at the paper mill. They're having some kind of special program tomorrow with out of town visitors and they ordered all these beautiful flower for the reception hall and conference room. Anything I can help you with?"

"No, I need to see him. He plays the harp at church. We'll both with the choir." She didn't want Marcia to know what she really wanted. She didn't want to give Joey advance notice, nor did she want Marcia to know. Seemed like everyone in town knew everyone's business—past, present, and future.

Maybe Harvey's right. Maybe they should just move out of Farley to another town—one where everyone would not know their business or try keeping up with everything they were doing.

"If it's really important, I can page him for you."

It was important. Very important.

"Yeah, that would be nice, if you don't mind."

"No problem at all." She went through a swinging door. She returned with a radio. She pressed a button. "Joey, you copy?" No response. "Joey, you there?"

"Yes, ma'am."

"Mary Ellen Forsman is here in the shop. She needs to talk to you. I'll put her on."

Put her on? That wasn't what she thought she meant. What did she think she meant? Tell him to come back to the shop so she could speak with him. Yeah, that's what she thought. Now what?

Marcia gave her the radio. She grinned. "Now you

had better not care who hears you—they say everyone can hear every thing on one of those things. You got any big secrets?" Then she chuckled as if she had said something funny. But Mary Ellen saw no humor in the remark. She smiled though.

She took the radio. "Joey?" Silence. "Joey."

"You have to push that little button and talk at the same time."

Mary Ellen pushed the button. "Joey, this is Mary Ellen." Silence. "Joey."

"Let go of the button." Mary Ellen let go.

A young male voice came over the line. "Oh, hi," Joey chirped.

"Hi, Joey. Uh...I need to ask you something."

"Sure."

"Uh..." Just what was she going to ask him?

"Are you going to ask him to play at your wedding," Marcia whispered.

"Play at my wedding?"

"You'll have to let go for his reply."

Mary Ellen looked at the radio. She still had the button pushed. Marcia gently lifted Mary Ellen's finger off the button, smiling sweetly at her.

"Oh, I would love to!"

Mary Ellen kept staring at the radio. That wasn't her question. She was just repeating Marcia's statement. Now what was she going to do? What could she do?

She handed the radio back to Marcia.

"Guess you've got a wedding to go to, young man," Marcia beamed.

"Ten-four," he replied jovially.

"I think that is so sweet of you. I know he is good with

that harp, but most people around here don't think about a harp, especially with a young guy playing it."

"Yeah—oh," she kept nodding her head, lost for words. Somewhere a thank you fell out of her mouth and she backed out of the shop with a small wave. Mary Ellen got into the car, a heavy sigh left her as her spirit fell. Oh, yeah…now what? She headed home with her spirit riding low on her shoulders.

Across town Harvey had been staring at the phone for the last twenty minutes. He felt his heart beating in the side of his neck just under his left ear. It thumped louder and stronger with each beat. He snapped the yellow #2 pencil between his thumb and fingers of his right hand. His left hand was still on the phone that he had slammed down when Gladys hung up.

Just a few more days and Gladys Forsman would be out of his life. It would take a little time, but not long. A lonely cold winter night with a pillow over her face should take care of her. They will never suspect. Alone in that big old house…she will just die quietly in her sleep.

He smiled. That gave him pleasure. Thinking about Gladys dying. He could see the horror on her face as he slipped into her bedroom and placed the soft pillow over her face. She couldn't be that strong. She never did anything for exercise—except sit on her butt watching those stupid soaps!

He twisted his fingers into a tight fist that he squeezed. Yes, Gladys Forsman was shortening her own time. There had been a time he would have taken Mary Ellen and left Farley, but the desire to squeeze that scrawny neck of that woman grew stronger. Besides—there was the money…he knew there was money. No one had ever mentioned money, but he could sniff that scent anytime and place. It was there. Just not seen.

He smiled. His thoughts drifting to how he would spend Gladys' money.

Chapter Twenty Nine

Sunday morning Joey Hanson told the choir the wonderful news. He was playing at Mary Ellen's wedding. When Mary Ellen smiled and nodded her head in agreement, the whole choir turned to her and in almost union stated 'how sweet' and 'isn't that nice'. It was almost as if they had practiced that instead of the Sunday morning special.

And there wasn't a darn thing she could do about it. The very person she thought had been sending her all the roses was now playing a harp at her wedding. Just where was the justice in all this? Gladys of course had not help in the situation at all. When Mary Ellen got back home, she told Gladys what had happened. She couldn't stop laughing. "Mother, please," she had pleaded with her, but the only response was just laughter.

Sunday night around six fifteen they sat at the dinner table. Baked ham lay in the platter. Baby limas and little red potatoes filled the bowls. Ears of tender yellow corn lay in a shallow white bowl. The ice clinked against the glasses as they drank their tea. They ate in silence except for the ice. Finally Harvey spoke.

"I heard you asked that young Hanson boy to play the harp." It was a statement.

Gladys snickered. Mary Ellen had told her all about the result of her confrontation with Joey. Harvey glanced her way, but Gladys kept eating.

"Yes. Yes, I did. I thought it would be a good experience for him. Seems like every one in town knows about it. That boy is so proud." Her voice was calm, steadfast.

When would all the lies end? She didn't want Harvey to know she suspected Joey. If he knew, he might say something. It was too late to say something now.

She didn't want any harp playing at her wedding. She didn't care for the harp. She didn't even like it in the church. She tolerated it. Now she had to tolerate it at her own wedding. Her mother thought it was so funny when she told her what had happened. She had laughed all weekend every time she looked at her. She just hoped she did not tell Harvey the truth.

"Pass me the limas please, Mary Ellen," Gladys said. Mary Ellen handed them to her without looking directly into her eyes. "These are good. You're a good cook, Mary Ellen—a very good cook."

"Thank you, mother." She had rather Gladys just didn't say anything since there was no way of knowing just what might come out of her mouth.

"You know I think harp music is so pretty. Maybe when I'm gone, you could have Joey play at my funeral?" She cut her eyes at Mary Ellen—smiled. "Seeing how you two are such good friends."

"Just because they play together at church don't mean they're that good of friends," Harvey said. "You planning on needing his service right away, Gladys?"

"You just never know about those kind of things."

"No, we don't," he said as he cut his ham with his fork.

He should use a knife, Gladys thought, then almost as

if he was reading her mind, he commented.

"Well, I should have used my knife. It makes things easier." He cut the meat. "You know," he said as he looked at Gladys, "there is so much power in a knife."

An icy smile touched his lips. Mary Ellen didn't see his frigid daring eyes on Gladys, but Gladys didn't miss it. A cold chill ran across her spine. But she refused to allow him to intimidate her.

"Well, Harvey, I'm glad to see that you are able to cut your own meat. I was beginning to wonder if you were one of these husbands who couldn't do anything." She threw her words at him, her eyes boring into his.

"Mother!"

"Well, I just wondered. I've never hear him talking about mowing the yard, or doing plumbing. I don't want you to be one of these wives who does everything around the house while the husband sits."

"I am sure a break for her from the last ten years of doing for—"

"Harvey, don't."

Gladys knew what he was saying without finishing the statement. He turned to Mary Ellen and smile. "Now tell me, dear, all about this friend of yours. Should I be jealous?"

Mary Ellen looked at her mother. Oh, it was going to blow. She knew it was. Harvey shouldn't have made the remark about the funeral. And mother about the work. It was a bomb just waiting to explode regardless of what she did or said. So why do anything? Why not just let them be at one another's throat and be done with it.

But she gave a weak smile as she replied, "No, Harvey, of course not."

"He's just a child, Harvey," Gladys informed. She took another bite of her beans. Her piece of ham was a little tough. Guess it was the way it was sliced.

Harvey watched as she wrestled with her ham. "Here," he said, "let me." He cut the ham as if she were a child. Gladys stared at him. Mary Ellen stared at both of them, waiting to see what would happen next, fearful of what it might be.

What's he up to? Gladys questioned, but she returned his smile. They were as two sparring partners in a ring, each throwing their best punch. She didn't know how to block this. Best to let him make another move before she darted out.

She waited. Nothing. This was hard. Too hard.

"Get that knife out of my plate!" she barked. "I'm not a child."

"Mother, he was just trying to help."

"If I so desire, I will pick up my food and eat it with my bare hands! I don't have to have someone cutting my food! I am not helpless!"

"No, of course not. Perhaps I overstepped." His voice soft, smooth.

She looked at Mary Ellen, who was sitting on the edge of her chair waiting to see what would happen next.

Gladys bit her tongue. On purpose. She could taste the warm salty blood. This was the man Mary Ellen had chosen. Not David. It would never be David. No yellow roses, no gifts would keep her from marrying this man. After all these years this was the man her beautiful daughter was going to give herself to, and there wasn't a darn thing she could do to stop it. Nothing.

She heard herself speak. She saw the surprise on Mary

Ellen's face, the way she was taken back when the words fell from her mouth.

"No, of course not, Harvey. I didn't mean to sound so rough." Lord Jesus, help me. You and I are going to have to have some long talks about this if I'm going to have to be nice to him. I think you need to repay me big time. This is a little beyond Christian love here.

She smiled. "After dinner, why don't you two sit in the front porch swing for a little while. It's a nice evening." Her tongue would be so sore in the morning. "I'll clear the table."

"That would be nice. I'll let you swing me, Mary Ellen," he chortled.

Like a young silly schoolgirl, he snickers, thought Gladys.

A few minutes later they went out side. She could hear the porch swing squeaking in the still warm gentle night. She picked up her plate and Mary Ellen's. But this time she also picked up Harvey's.

Chapter Thirty

There wasn't a rose on the doorstep Monday morning. Nor did a gift come. At ten thirty, Gladys informed Mary Ellen she had an appointment she had to keep. She would be taking the car.

"Taking the car? You haven't driven that car since daddy passed!"

"Then I guess I'm over due. I don't want to take a taxi."

"I could drive you if you want."

"No. I don't."

Mary Ellen hesitated. Where was her mother going? Wasn't she going to tell? She wanted to ask, but feared she might be told it was none of her business. She was surprised when her mother offered to clear the table last night. Surprised to find her in the kitchen this morning with something besides a bowl of cold cereal. It was strange to see her mother in front of the stove with a skillet in her hand.

The eggs were good, though. She hadn't lost her touch for cooking. How often she would use it was the question.

"Mother, I've been thinking. I don't want you to be all alone here once I get married. I thought maybe you might think about taking in a boarder. That way there would be someone here with you."

Gladys set the empty skillet in the sink, sat her plate of eggs and sausage on the table across from Mary Ellen. She opened the refrigerator and removed a pitcher of orange juice. From the white cabinet, she took down a 12oz clear water glass and poured it full of juice. This she sat next to her plate. Then she took catsup from the refrigerator when she replaced the juice.

"Did you want juice?"

"Yes, please." Wonder why she didn't ask before she put it back in the fridge.

Gladys sat down. She began to eat her egg. Mary Ellen peered at her. The juice.

"Well, I guess I can get my own." Why ask if she wasn't going to get it for her.

"Get your own what?"

"Juice. You asked if I wanted juice."

"Oh, I did?" Gladys replied as if bewildered.

"You don't remember?"

"Of course, I do. I just thought you must think I'm a little off in the head or something since I'm not capable of staying by myself."

"I didn't mean it that way. I just thought you wouldn't want to be alone. You've never lived alone."

Gladys smiled. "No, I haven't. Won't that be something," she said with a touch of excitement.

Mary Ellen poured her juice. "Well, I don't know if that's the right statement or not. It can be very lonely."

"And how would you know?"

"I'm just trying to help, mother, that's all."

Gladys smiled. "I know." The smile thawed the

atmosphere. "Don't you think I can't take care of myself? I can."

Mary Ellen sat back down. She took a deep drink of juice. It emptied the glass. Hers was a small juice glass.

Gladys smiled again. The smile softened the lines around her mouth. "I should have just given you the pitcher. You have always loved juice."

Mary Ellen ran her finger around the empty glass. "And you. Always loved you and daddy." Tears touched her eyelashes. "It's hard to believe in just four days I won't be living here any more. That the life we had is over."

"I know, baby."

"I mean I'm glad...glad I'm getting married...I just always thought when I got married...daddy would be here...you wouldn't be alone...that everything would be different."

"So did I. But we take what we've got and go from there. I'll be ok. Besides, I'm working on a surprise for you."

"Oh, really? What?"

"On your wedding day. I'll tell you then."

"Has it got anything to do with where you are going this morning?"

"Eat your eggs."

At twelve-thirty Gladys pulled Norbert's Thunderbird back into the garage. It had been a very profitable morning. She was excited. Mary Ellen was going to be surprised—no, shocked—come Saturday. Oh, she wished she had done this years ago!

She went through the back door. Mary Ellen should be home—probably working on those lessons. How she could work with those kids she just didn't understand. Half the time they didn't want to practice. Some of them too shy to want to be in recitals. Their mothers had to force them. And some of them just didn't have any talent at all. It had to be their mother's idea for them to take lessons.

Why would a parent insist a child learn an instrument that the child detested? If he likes drums—give him drums. Not a piano.

Most boys would like drums, she bet. Huh! She'd rather play drums!

She laid her purse on the kitchen table. There was no indication that anyone was home. Maybe Mary Ellen was out with her bridesmaids. There were just a few more days.

She glanced out the kitchen window into the back yard and saw her. Sitting on the edge of the fishpond, her hand dragging through the water. Her shoulders drooped slightly. What was Mary Ellen thinking about? She seemed to be in such deep thought. Did she have any doubts about Saturday? If only there might be the slightest possibility that girl would call off this foolish wedding.

What if her fears about Harvey were true? She still wondered about Mildred. An old dog after a bone wouldn't be any worse than she was about this but she couldn't help it. Stranger things have happen. Men do kill their wives!

Why, when she was a kid, there was some guy who killed his wife and buried her under a fishpond. One very much like the one Mary Ellen is sitting at right now. She had teased Norbert when he said he was putting in a fishpond, but he said that wasn't something to kid about— that poor woman buried under a fishpond right in her own back yard for three years while her family searched for her. Nothing to jest about.

And he was right!

She wanted to go to Mary Ellen, but she didn't know what to say to her. Instead she watched her for a few minutes, then she couldn't stand it any longer. The poor child looked so doleful.

Gladys opened the back door. "Mary Ellen," she called across the yard. Mary Ellen looked up and gave a slight wave. "Come here."

Slowly Mary Ellen rose

"Baby," she said as she gathered her daughter into her arms. "What's wrong?"

"I just don't know any more, mom. I wish David hadn't left. I wish…oh, I wish so many things." She laid her head on her mother's shoulder and cried. Slowly Gladys closed the door and they went into the house.

"Sit down," Gladys said as she pulled out a kitchen chair. She poured two glasses of ice tea, set them on the table, and sat down. "Ok, tell me what do you want to do. Not what you feel like you should do. But be honest with yourself and say it."

"I know you want me to say I won't marry Harvey…"

"Wait a minute. That's not what I said. I said what do you want."

"That's the problem. I honestly don't know. Until the roses, David coming to town, I knew. I was excited about my wedding, but it just seems as if everything has turned upside down."

"What does David coming to town have anything to do with what you're feeling now?"

"It's just…" The ringing phone broke her words. She left her thought and went to the phone. "Oh, hi. Glad you called. Needed to hear your voice." She waited. "No nothing wrong."

Again she was silent. A soft smile toughed her lips. Gladys knew who was on the phone and she also knew the moment had passed. Harvey had pulled her back to him.

When Harvey came over for dinner, Mary Ellen seemed like herself, but Gladys still noticed sadness in her eyes.

Chapter Thirty One

"Ok, so Harvey didn't kill his wife," Gladys said to the reflection in the mirror. "Or if he did, it can't be proven, and maybe he didn't. Maybe you wanted it to be true just so Mary Ellen would not marry him. Your baby girl will marry this man and if you are to keep peace in the family, you must accept Harvey Broyhill as your son-in-law." She pointed the brush in her hand at the mirror. "Are you listening to me, Gladys?" After seeing the sadness in Mary Ellen's eyes, she knew that she had to make peace with Harvey.

"Mother, who are you talking to?"

"Oh, what? No one."

Mary Ellen stood at the bottom of the stairs. She had just come in from getting Harvey's ring. Every time she planned to pick it up, something else came up. "I just thought I heard you talking. You ok?"

Gladys moved to the top of the stairs. "Yeah, baby— I'm fine. You get the ring?"

"Yes." Mary Ellen held up the small box. "It's real pretty."

Gladys moved down the stairs. "There wasn't anything on the porch this morning, was there?"

"No, thank goodness." Mary Ellen sighed. "I wonder

who and why? Have you talked to Mrs. Petrie? Wonder if she's heard anything from David."

Gladys came down the stairs, her hand on the rail, walking slowly as she talked. "No, guess he's in Africa by now. She said he was leaving right away."

Mary Ellen went to her piano, placed the small box on it, picked up her books. "Guess I need to get ready for this afternoon." Without looking at her mother, she said, "Don't forget we have a rehearsal Friday night. Dinner afterward with Harvey and his family. His sons are coming in on Thursday. Harvey said he probably won't be over this week since he had so many things to do to get ready for their visit. That he would meet us at the church on Friday night at six."

She never did look up and Gladys had plenty of remarks just sitting on the end of her tongue, but she reminded herself of her new found attitude. Hard as it was, she kept her mouth shut.

On Friday night Gladys and Mary Ellen arrived at the church at five-thirty. Mary Ellen wanted to make sure the reception hall was decorated for Saturday's event. Gladys thought everything looked fine, but Mary Ellen kept moving the flower arrangements around on one of the tables as if she could not place it just as she wanted. When she was finished, Gladys couldn't see any difference in it. When they went into the church, Harvey and his family was there. The four bridesmaids were also waiting for her. The women gathered around Mary Ellen, excited, all talking at once.

They're more excited than I am, Mary Ellen thought. Tomorrow I will be a married woman and my bridesmaids are the ones who are laughing and chattering like teenagers.

Two weeks ago I was just like them. Before the roses—before David. Who sent those flowers? What did they mean? Anything? Probably not.

"Darling." Harvey gather her hand into his, pulling her to him. "Tomorrow we will finally be married." He leaned over and kissed her cheek, then he smiled at her.

"Yes," she replied, but she wasn't thinking about tomorrow. Instead she was thinking about the kiss. It stirred nothing inside her. Why? Before all he had to do was smile at her, touch her hand. Now, the thought of tomorrow or a kiss stirred nothing within her.

They took their places. Gladys and Mary Ellen walked down the aisle. The preacher asked who gives the bride and Gladys said she did. Each person performed perfectly. Harvey's son Jeffrey stood in for his dad. The wedding director did not want the groom and bride repeating any vows or standing before the preacher.

After the practice, the wedding director beamed, "Oh, yes. Perfect. This wedding will come on without a hitch."

Gladys sighed. At least she had her own plans.

Chapter Thirty Two

Gladys bounded through the front door. Mary Ellen was standing on the third step from the bottom.

"Where have you been?" she demanded. "Don't you realize we should have left for the church ten minutes ago!" In her hand was her make up case. The dress was at the church. "Did you forget the plan was for us to be there in time to get ready? I don't want to walk down the aisle in my hair roller and no make up!"

"There's plenty of time."

"Ok, Mom, ok. If you say so. You coming with me? Did you leave the car in the drive?"

Gladys grinned. "Sure did." Then she boldly threw open the front door. Mary Ellen gasped, stopping in mid-steps as she walked onto the front porch. "Isn't she a beau!" Gladys said, then she laughed. "Prettiest little number every made. Been wanting that little baby since I was eighteen years old."

"What is it?"

"The prettiest thing that ever had wheels! A 1957 Ford Thunderbird. The color is called Precious Teal—'course most folks would just say teal."

"When? Why? Why on earth did you buy that? What

about daddy's car?"

"Sold it. I knew you wouldn't need it. Huh, you will be lucky if Harvey lets you drive a car."

Mary Ellen stared at her mother. There was no way she was going to argue with her today. But a 1957 Ford Thunderbird!

Never would she have pictured her mother wanting such a car. She was astounded at her! There were no words for this moment. She didn't know whether to be proud her mother was finally doing something, or be alarmed she was deranged.

"Well, let's hurry up, baby girl," Gladys said. "No sense in being late for your big moment." She scooted up the stairs, returning with a few items tossed into a satchel. "I think this is everything I need." She dug around in the bag. "Curling iron, panty hoses, a little makeup and …oh yeah, I forgot my slip. Let me run back upstairs for that."

Mary Ellen was still on the front porch. "Mother, you won't need it. Your dress is lined, and we're going to be late…oh please…"

Gladys leapt down the stone steps. "I guess you're right." She was at the car before Mary Ellen. "No sense in being an old fuddy-duddy any way." Then mischievously she asked, "You want to drive? Lots more fun when you're in the driver's seat and not just riding—like you were in David's car."

"No, Mother, I do not. Nor do I want to hear about David. I guess you and he can compare cars." She didn't want to argue. Or defend herself about David. There was no David; he left town just like he did fifteen years ago. Without giving her a thought or bothering to say good-bye. So why did her mother have to be so cruel bringing up his name?

She got into the passenger side of the little teal car. The interior had white leather seats. She had to admit it was nice. Well—she wouldn't say that aloud, she thought as she ran her hand discreetly over the seat.

Gladys threw her small bag behind the front seat, then got behind the wheel. "Oh this is going to be a blast!"

Mary Ellen looked at her mother in disbelief. That woman had never talked this way before. Her mother was no longer acting anything like her mother.

Skillfully Gladys backed the little teal car into the street and sped away toward the church. Alice Petrie pulled her Plymouth out of the garage. She saw the little teal car leaving Gladys' drive but wasn't sure who was driving. Probably some of Gladys' out of town family. She wondered if they were as crazy as Gladys.

Maybe not. Mary Ellen certainly wasn't anything like Gladys. She will make a fine wife. Not a doubt in her mind, but was surprised when she took up with that Harvey fellow. He seemed so old to her.

Mary Ellen had never looked her age—at least Alice didn't think she did. But she guessed most young people didn't look at things like she did. They looked at every little line today as a crack carved into their face. Age can truly enhance a woman when given a chance. But Mary Ellen had almost a baby doll look, that fine china-doll look that most girls never have. She was pretty, smart, talented.

Yes, Mary Ellen was a fine young woman—but that mother of hers was a complete different story. She still just couldn't figure that one out. Maybe Mary Ellen was adopted. That would explain a lot of things.

Chapter Thirty Three

"I'm sorry, sir, but you will have to go into the balcony. There is no more room. They are ready to begin their vows," the lady told him. She was the director of this wedding and last minute guest could just wait outside for all she cared. There were a few seats upstairs, but she didn't really care if late arrivals got a seat or not. To be so rude as to arrive late for a wedding. What next? Late for a funeral and disturb the bereaved mourners

He stood there. What was he doing here? She was getting married. There was nothing he could do now. Why even be here? It should be him by her side.

"Sir, you can not stand here," the director whispered.

David moved to the balcony, taking the steps two at a time. Once he got to the top, he stopped and stood next to the rail, staring down on the ceremony below.

He couldn't see her face. Upon her head was a sheer white lace headpiece. She was covered in a long white wedding gown. A long train lay behind her. And he knew she was beautiful.

The preacher asked who gave this woman. Gladys replied unpretentiously. Then she moved away and Harvey stood beside his bride.

"Dearly beloved, we are gathered here in the sight of God and man to join this couple in holy matrimony. This is a sacred moment and should not be entered into lightly," the preacher said. He looked at the couple, smiling warmly at them. Then he looked up over the crowd and said words that David had not really thought about.

"Is there anyone here who objects to this union, let him speak now or forever..."

"El." The voice boomed from the upper room. Again he cried, "El, marry me!"

Then David did something that later would be the talk of Farley for many years to come. He climbed on the rail of the balcony, and leaped toward the chandelier. He caught the chain that suspended the light fixture, and swung his body forward toward the startled bride and groom. The congregation gasped as David dropped from the chandelier, landing almost at Mary Ellen's feet. Jumping up, he rushed toward her.

He dropped to one knee. "Marry me, El," he quickly said. Then in a softer, calm, loving tone as he took her hand, he whispered, "Will you marry me, El?" His eyes gazed into hers.

"YAHOO!" Gladys shouted as she swirled her lace handkerchief over her head as if she was riding the open range and heading the steers onward.

Mary Ellen's mouth fell open. Harvey swung at David, punching him in the mouth, which knocked David over.

David touched his bloody mouth. Without getting up, he repeated the words, "Will you marry me, El?"

Gladys sprang from her second pew seat when Harvey

punched David. She bolted toward the men. She had to defend David against Harvey. Not that David couldn't take care of himself, she knew, but all the tension of the last few weeks was boiling beneath the surface. Might as well mix it with Harvey too.

Gladys shoved Harvey away from David. Looking back at David, she encouraged, "Ask her again, David, ask her again."

Harvey pushed Gladys aside. He moved toward David, who was only looking at Mary Ellen, who was staring at David with her hand over her mouth. She was overwhelmed.

When Harvey pulled back his fist to hit David again, Alice was there. Alice Petrie had been sitting three rows back. She grasped his arm, and with a voice as cold as the Northern winds on a crisp winter morning, she spoke.

"No one touches my Davie—no one."

She always viewed herself as a fine Christian woman and would never truly do anyone wrong if it could be helped. But no one hits her David. Not when he was a child and not now as an adult. If he wanted to swing on the church's chandelier, then so be. If he wanted to ask Mary Ellen to marry him, it was about time.

Harvey looked into the cold gray eyes. He knew he could whip the old broad—but he just wasn't sure what her retaliation would be. He lowered his fist, and turned to speak to Mary Ellen. But she wasn't by his side any longer. He caught a glimpse of a long white wedding train just as the front door closed.

"Ohhhh!" cried Mary Ellen as she stood outside the church. "How? I can't believe this! How did you do this?" In front of her was David's car, but cardboard was fastened to the car, creating the image of a silver spacecraft. Across the side was written Galley 4000, and below that was written The Blue Eagles. "Our spaceship!" She whirled around. "Oh, David!" she cried as she threw her arms around his neck.

"Come on," he said. He went to the driver's side, "Come on, El. Here's your control panel." When Mary Ellen saw the steeling wheel, again she cried out. The wheel was covered with aluminum foil. "Hop in. We've got places to go, worlds to see, and a life time of love."

Mary Ellen eased behind the wheel of their spaceship. David closed the car door, and hurried around to the other side, slipped in beside her.

As they sped out of Farley, Mary Ellen asked, "Where are we going?"

"To Africa," David grinned. "We will honeymoon in Africa."

"That will be nice," Mary Ellen replied, as her wedding veil blew off her head and floated behind them in the air like a free dove soaring to freedom, then rested softly on the grassy knoll beside the street. "A honeymoon in Africa." David patted her knee. This time she didn't blush.

The guest rushed from the church just in time to see Mary Ellen's veil flying through the air. Some were laughing; others were puzzled; and some felt sorry for Harvey who just stood there watching the spaceship speed out of town.

This was not the way he had planned their wedding day. Mary Ellen would have made him a good obedient wife or so he thought until two weeks ago. It was good he saw her true colors. Next time he would pick his bride out very carefully. There would not be another Mildred, or a Mary Ellen. Nor would there be a fancy wedding—they would go to the justice of peace!

Gladys walked over to her '58 Ford Thunderbird. She opened the door, and called to Alice Petrie.

"You need a ride home?" Might as well be civil to the old bat since they were now family.

"Oh no, I have the Plymouth." She turned to say something to Harvey. What she wasn't for sure, but she didn't want any ill feelings. That just wasn't Christian. But he was no longer standing in the crowd. He was getting into his car. Gloria had her hand on his arm as if to comfort him. They both got into his car and left. His two sons from Denver—Denton—wherever—got into a car with their family behind their father, and Gloria's husband and children got into another car. The Broyhills had left the church.

Alice turned back to Gladys. Gladys was getting into her little Thunderbird. It surprised her to see Gladys in that thing. Why on earth did she buy that? Oh well—better her than me, she thought. At least someone had to keep a little sanity around here since Mary Ellen wasn't around to keep her mother in tow. Would be a full time job seeing after Gladys, considering how she was.

Then Alice thought about all that food. "Gladys, what about the food? You can't just leave!"

"Have a party. There's plenty to celebrate."

"But aren't you going to stay?"

Gladys laughed. "Oh, no! I've got a plane to catch!"

"A plane! What are you talking about? What plane?"

Gladys laughed. Oh, how she enjoyed rattling Alice's cage. Poor thing. She needed to get out of those flowerbeds and have a little adventure in her life. Maybe she should have let her help with the yellow rose mystery. But she couldn't see Alice climbing in and out of a dumpster in the hot pursuit of hot clues. Or talking to the police. Poor boring Alice. Then she smiled as she said her next words. Oh, how sweet life had suddenly become! "I'm leaving for Paris at seven—tonight."

Alice gasped. "Tonight! Paris!"

"Yap. No sense in staying home all the time," she laughed as she pulled the little teal colored Thunderbird out of the parking lot.

Epilogue

Alice Petrie stood in the doorway of her hothouse. Soon it would be summer. The days were longer now; spring was in full force. She had all of her plants to move into the yard—transplanting pots of petunias to the beds, and setting out the tall banana plant. Perhaps it would bear fruit along with the orange tree this year.

She had received a post card from Gladys, saying how exciting Paris was. It was a pretty card. But what warmed her heart was the letter she received from Mary Ellen and David. They had gotten married in Kenya, standing on a beach. The sun was rising and the warm ocean washed across their bare feet as they said their vows.

She smiled. Perhaps there would be a baby in the near future. She was so happy David and Mary Ellen were finally together. They should have married years ago. They were always so close—at least until those teen years.

She kept showing Mary Ellen all of David's newspaper clippings, hoping it would spark that old friendship between them again. Then David left Farley—got married. It seemed as if it was all over. She had accepted her new daughter-in-law, but she always loved Mary Ellen. And when David left, and they divorced, she so wanted him to come home! Oh, she just knew the young love would draw them together, but David wouldn't come home.

Then Harvey arrived on the scene. There was just something about Harvey—something that caused her to feel Mary Ellen was making a horrible mistake. Even if she didn't marry David, she didn't need Harvey. He just wasn't right for her.

But what could she do—then this crazy idea hit her. And when David came home...

She smiled. It had all been so easy once they were together again.

Her eyes traveled across the room to the corner. That one was meant for the front yard. But it had served a better purpose than just beautifying the front yard. She moved to the far corner. It was such a shame destroying its early blooms. But there had been no other way. There would be more later.

She reached her hand up to the one bloom still on the bush. It was the prettiest one. She leaned over and inhaled deeply. The fragrance was sweet. Its soft velvet petals bathed in the warm morning sun causing them to be as pure gold. Such a beautiful rose. There was nothing prettier than a yellow rose.

The End

Author's Note: Thank you for buying *Petals of Deception*. I do hope you enjoyed the read and that the characters warmed your heart. I have other books that I have written. **Under The Fish Pond** is based on a true story, while **Back To Midnight** has a young deputy by the name of Nathan Oneal, the same character in this book. I hope you will consider these books as well. Again, I thank you for buying *Petals of Deception*.

Glenda Yarbrough

Made in the USA
Middletown, DE
06 December 2016